GOBBLEMOUTH

Ted Lamb

By the same author

The Penguin Book of Fishing, Penguin guides to sea and freshwater fishing in Britain, The Bait Book, fishing stories Looking for Lucie and Brassribs (also published together with Gobblemouth as The Brightwell Trilogy), novels Gansalaman's Gold and Match of the Day; novelette The Box; and children's story Monty and the Mauler. Poetry works on Kindle are One Last Cast and The Ballad of Sally Stardust.

Copyright Ted Lamb 2017

Published by Edict Editorial, 21 Arthur Bliss Gardens, Cheltenham, Glos GL50 2LN

Tel: 01242 572873.

Email: edictserv@yahoo.co.uk

For Caspar and Sarah

Chapter 1

"Oh... my...God!"

Like the other five, Michael Tipton stared in stunned disbelief - they had come back from the village restaurant in high spirits, but at their temporary farmyard transit camp the mood shifted close to panic: in the middle of France the padlocked gate had been broken into and their giant fish transporter truck had simply vanished. More importantly, 8,000 valuable infant arctic char and 50 or so breeding-size rainbow trout had gone with it, and along with them the only fish that really mattered to unofficial big fish specialist Mark Kendal (and most of the others for that matter) - Gobblemouth, an enormous catfish. It looked as if the whole expedition, let alone the aptly-named Quest for the Crimson Trout, was well and truly dead in the water - if that wasn't too unfortunate a metaphor.

Tipton, major sponsor of the trip and very much the elder statesman (titled, to boot), was white-faced.

"Jeeze!" His younger brother, Giles, provided an unselfconscious Australian comment.

Young Vicky Price started to sob, and Mike Cook moved quickly to her side, concerned. Truck driver Derek Jones, normally not short of a succinct comment or two, seemed simply dumbstruck, while his navigator and co-driver Pedro DeAvila looked more agitated than all of them put together - there was more to the dark little man's edgy behaviour so far on this trip than met the eye, Kendal had already decided. He had his theories, but so far hadn't got to the bottom of it.

"Well," he said, adding his own contribution to the situation, "What now?"

Half an hour later, back in the village, they managed to rouse the mayor. Grumpy, he reluctantly telephoned the gendarmes for them. But as Tipton climbed into the Range Rover with Kendal and Mike Cook to lead the police back to the farmyard scene-of-crime, the young man suddenly spoke a few brief words that brought an even deeper chill.

"Can anyone smell frying fish?"

He wasn't mucking around...

***

All adventures have to start somewhere and this one had its origins almost 20 years earlier in a part of eastern Europe remarkable then as now for tribal mistrusts and constant fallings out between not only different ethnic groups but also adjacent villages and even next door neighbours. The inhabitants were a thoroughly quarrelsome lot with most households armed to the teeth, if not with carefully stashed ancient firearms then with sabres and wicked hooked daggers that had probably first seen service during the Crusades.

While the huge 20th century wars between nations had raged as an overlay to all this bitter infighting, throughout the whole troubled arena there threaded another completely detached nation, wanderers, always on the move, tinkers, fortune-tellers, peg-sellers, tricksters, thieves and travelling show folk, never allowing themselves to settle or be drawn into one side or another at whatever level. National boundaries meant nothing to them, nor indeed land - why bother to fight over anything so insignificant?

Not long after the cessation of a particularly savage regional scrap one of these small travelling groups found itself on the banks of a fine broad river that flowed from beyond Vienna in the North to the Black Sea in the East: the Danube. In the 'real' world people like these travellers had a reputation for laziness and even skulduggery but this was far from the case here: maintaining independence took hard work, and to suppose quick, dark little Zofia was idling her time away with a fishing net at the water's edge was a long way short of accurate or even being fair to her. In fact, she was catching some of the prizes for next week's shows, when her family would be moving gradually to the west now that the fighting was over, fitting in with her Dada's plans to join a larger part of the clan in faraway England, which Zofia had never visited before. At the centre of the English venture there was to be an important clan marriage, and the family had received a call to join the reunion and festivities, all of which was very exciting to look forward to for a girl of 11.

"Ach!"

Zofia swept coils of her black hair aside to inspect her catch: she had drawn in a netfull of wriggling, baby black catfish. Really she was after bitterling, tiny iridescent little fish which adapted well to goldfish bowls and provided the necessary glitter to make attractive prizes for the wide-eyed folk, mostly young, who came to Dada's hoop-la stall in the hope of throwing a wooden ring over expensive-looking scent bottles which she knew contained nothing more than coloured water. The boys threw to impress the girls with their skills, the girls threw because they dearly wanted to gain the treasured allure of the bottles' promised contents. Mostly the punters went away empty-handed, unable to throw one of the rings cleverly enough to make it drop over the square base on which the bottle sat: it's a game that looks easy but one where the banker almost always wins. Thwarted, players would wander away, perhaps to the exotic looking tent where Zofia's mother, Anja, told fortunes, her black eyes glittering mysteriously behind a gauzy blue and crimson silk scarf dotted with gold stars.

But fish were fish, and catfish had been on the prize menu before now when bitterling, or goldfish 'liberated' from some local park or the garden of some great house, were hard to come by: Dada, dark, stocky and good humoured, was always able to persuade the rare winner of such treats that a catfish was something extraordinary and wonderful that would bring good luck to the house in which it was kept. If the winners were disappointed in receiving a rather common and not very colourful fish presented in a small transparent waterproof bag of water rather than the glamorous prize they had hoped for, they hardly ever showed it. Once, when Zofia expressed the opinion that the fish might not be very well looked after considering no care and maintenance advice came with a win, Dada told her not to worry, as most of them went straight back into the river under strict parental direction rather than being another mouth for the household to feed. Or, indeed, something the parents themselves wanted to get rid of since they would inevitably find themselves looking after these baby monsters once their children lost interest in keeping a pet. And monsters was what these ugly little fish would inevitably become, for they ate voraciously and grew rapidly - and woe betide any goldfish or other ornamental fish that shared their bowl or tank.

"Anyway, fairs are really nothing at all to do with winning prizes," Dada added with one of his mischief-smiles. "At least not the prizes you are thinking of. You will see this in time."

Zofia always found the visiting village children a curious lot and rather dull: they had to stay always in the same place, and they had to go to school rather than learning all that was important enough to learn from their mothers and fathers. In fact, while she fished, she had just been considering how lucky she was to have such a carefree life and the prospect of an exciting trip to England rather than stay in the frankly very ordinary nearby settlement. A low double-whistle broke into this reverie. The signal!

It was Dada's secret message to pack up and leave. Sometimes (depending on its intensity) it meant the nearby community was growing tired of this particular fair and would not be spending much more of their time and money there. But sometimes it also meant that trouble was brewing, somebody getting upset for some reason by this band of 'fly-by-nights' in their midst. When this was the case the whistle seemed, as now, especially urgent. With another "Ach!" Zofia picked up her net and bucket of fish and headed straight back to the camp.

7

'Striking' (packing up) the fair was already well under-way. She found Dada dealing with the intricately-hinged hoopla stall table, which folded tightly into one flat piece. Her mother's tent was already rolled-up around its tent poles and tied tightly with the guy-ropes. They owned a little high-sided motor truck, and it was an easy matter to place all the show paraphernalia aboard and hitch their small caravan on behind while around them the half dozen other sideshows and attractions that made up the little fair were being packed up just as quickly.

Dada looked down at her, calm but businesslike.

"Up girl, quick!"

Zofia barely had time to clamber over her mother's legs, still clutching her fish bucket , and sit on the engine cover between her parents, before they were off, past a bunch of angry-looking village louts with sticks who shied stones after them. They drove quickly out of a maze of back lanes and byways and were soon meshing into the after-work traffic of the highway.

Her mother gave her a dazzling smile: Zofia could tell she was glad to be on the road again. It was their way of life. Being rooted was not in their nature.

And Gobblemouth (though he had not yet so been named), squirming among a little group of fellow baby catfish at the bottom of a bucket clasped between Zofia's knees, had started his long journey to England.

***

Two months afterwards, in the late summer of that year at the latter end of the twentieth century, Zofia and her family split away from the rest of the little travelling fair on the French coast near Calais and headed towards the port. Dada left them in the Gare Maritime for some time while he went off to do some wheeler-dealing carrying a precious tin box of their important papers under his arm. Dada never had any time for such niceties as pre-booking a Channel crossing.

Everything he ever did was decided on the spur of the moment, and anything he ever wanted to achieve could be sorted out by quick-witted charm and the occasional dollop of cash into the right hands. He was shortly back with tickets for their passage the next morning and for the truck and their home, which was taking the place reserved for a tourist's caravan which had broken down and would not make the port for days. Just as exciting for Zofia was a grilled sardine supper - how even the smell made her feel hungry! - in a harbourside restaurant, with a bottle of Cotes du Rhone for her parents, a little splash of it in her own glass of water as a special treat. Her mother's eyes shone as they talked about the next day's adventure: Zofia could see that she was every bit as excited as she was herself.

On board the next morning, after clambering up and through a maze of companionways and staircases, she was simply amazed. The ship was huge, a palace. It had fine bars and restaurants, a cinema, even shops! It was far, far more glamorous than anything she had ever imagined. After Dada had taken her to a big wall diagram of the ship's insides and pointed out how she could find her way back to their window seats, she was allowed to explore on her own, inside and out. And on this fine but breezy day she watched in awe as men on the quay loosed the huge ropes which held the ferry in place. With a long, brave blast of its foghorn, the ship started gradually to move away. People on the dockside waved as they slipped past, and Zofia waved back. Soon they were in open water, the first time she had ever been afloat on the sea, and the engines took on a purposeful tone while the whole ship vibrated with their power.

It was a smooth crossing and Zofia delighted in every moment of it. The topmost deck was her favourite place, and from it she saw other ships, birds diving for fish and even, she fancied, a dolphin. The rushing spray speeding aside was mesmerising, and it was while she was staring down at this that there was a sudden stir among the group of travellers at the ship's bow. She went forward to find out what is was about and saw they were pointing eagerly ahead and talking excitedly. Pushing through them to the rail, she saw that a

9

long, low line of white cliffs had appeared. They were getting close to England.

After driving off the ship, Dada said: "I bet they'll stop us." Sure enough, as they approached the Customs area they were waved aside from the line of departing traffic and guided into a large, open-ended shed where they were signalled to stop. A man stuck his head through Dada's window.

"Any livestock, plants or other agricultural produce?" he said, pushing a picture-card of banned imports under Dada's nose, "Sprits? Tobacco?".

"No," said Dada, one unobserved hand pushing the hem of Zofia's skirt over the bucket between her legs containing the last half-dozen catfish. "Nothing at all to declare."

Dada looked and sounded assured , but all the same the customs officers insisted on looking over everything in the truck bed after pulling back its cover, and then looking carefully through the caravan from top to bottom while her untrusting mother stood watch over them.

She returned rolling her deep black eyes, a smile playing at the corners of her mouth even though she was trying to keep a serious face for appearances, at least until they were clear away. "They turned over every drawer," she said, scandalised, when they were finally ushered on their way. "I thought they were going to start unscrewing all the panels."

Out of the port at last, they stopped in an abandoned garage forecourt for the night and then Dada drove them westwards while heading upcountry, picking a line of villages from an old road map. In each of these he looked, eagle-eyed, out of his open window, scanning any coloured posters on lamp-posts or on boarded-up empty buildings as they drove past.

Eventually, driving into a small town, he stopped by a poster advertising a travelling fair, said, "Aha!" and looked excited. Using

English - still strange words to Zofia - he stuck his head out of the window and asked a passer-by where the recreation ground was. Soon they found a large green field and, wonder of wonders, it held a little group of fairground vehicles not unlike the one they had recently left in France. After questioning some of the people there and driving from one vehicle to another he spotted a stout figure, slapped on the brakes with a jolt that nearly spilled all Zofia's fish, leapt out of the cab and embraced the man.

"George!"

Dada's face was face red with emotion.

"Marco!" the man hugged him back.

Dada beckoned Zofia and her mother out of the truck.

"Come and meet my cousin!"

***

Nobody, but nobody celebrates a wedding like the travelling community. A month of little four-day fairs with Cousin George and his relatives had brought Zofia and her family to the enormous field hired for the occasion. In the midst of it all a very beautiful woman had married an extremely handsome man, a union of Purrum and Petulengro but to Zofia, born a Balorengre but nevertheless related to the Petulengro, that was only one small part of a week of partying, because she had fallen in love.

She was now nearly 12, while the object of her infatuation (he did not immediately know of this crush) was 13, possibly even 14, fair but sunburned and a good deal taller than she was. Generally Georgie Lee was reckoned to be a very useful member of the fair team, helping out with everything about the site while it was working. But for now, like her, he had time on his hands while the adults were celebrating. The name 'Georgie Lee' tripped easily off the tongue but 'Lee' was an adopted name and he was a Purrum among Romanies, hence his presence at the wedding. Customarily the tribes kept their Romany names for dealings among themselves.

Haunting the site for a chance to catch a glimpse of her blue-dungareed hero and generally moody whenever she was unable to go out meant Zofia had started to neglect her bucket-aquarium guests. There remained but one of the catfish, which now shared his bucket of weedy water with ten three-inch goldfish, just changing colour from infant black to orange. Zofia had clandestinely netted the new arrivals from a park pond. When prizes were offered the catfish was steadfastly overlooked in favour of goldfish.

Too shy to make a direct approach to the object of her attention, Zofia found herself joining in with the other girls who were adept at throwing cheeky taunts to all the boys, and to Georgie in particular - he was clearly a favourite. And didn't he know it, drawing himself up to swagger past the bunch of harpies with his nose in the air while they sang "*Georgie, Porgie, pudd'n and pie, kissed the girls and made them cry*" in mocking tones. Did he catch and hold Zofia's eye for longer than he held any of the others? She thought so...

Up to the wedding the catfish had been living quite royally on chopped up earthworms collected and prepared by their very unsqueamish minder, who also raided ants nests for the eggs and larvae favoured by the goldfish. But a couple of days before the wedding party was about to break up and the families headed off on their separate ways, the rapidly growing four-inch catfish was suffering from the effects of Zofia's undeclared love. In short he was close to starving.

Then, the day before Zofia and her family were leaving themselves, Zofia woke to find that Georgie's caravan was missing; his family had departed at dawn, and the only progress their affair had made to that date was a few seconds of catching prolonged glances, and both blushing deeply at what they read in each other's faces.

"What's up girl?" inquired Dada, always attuned to her moods whenever he wasn't otherwise engaged. "Look like you've eaten an addled egg."

"Nothing," she said, avoiding his gaze. But then, a few minutes later: "I wonder where Georgie Lee's family are going. Are we going to join them there?"

Dada looked at his daughter closely, shaking his head. "Shouldn't think so," he said truthfully. "We shall be heading back to the Continent soon." Nevertheless, he had read the signs there, plain enough to see: he knew that look, and in times to come Georgie Lee and others like him had better watch out.

"But I want to stay here in England," she protested, "it's lovely." Indeed it was, with autumn beginning to colour the leaves.

But Dada rejoined: "You wouldn't like it." He had spent many winters in England in his boyhood, and there were far kinder places to see the worst months out. "Look," he said, smiling, "you'd better go look at those fish before they get sick. I'd say they need a water change and some food."

It was when she was checking them that she discovered there remained but nine goldfish, while the catfish seemed rather smugly tubbier. She frowned. Something had to be done about that, and for the first time in quite a while she forgot all about Georgie Lee.

***

They had been travelling for two or three hours on minor country roads when Zofia suddenly called out: "Stop!"

Dada pulled into the lay-by they were approaching and looked at her, cross.

"What?"

Zofia pointed down the sloping field to their left, where the silvery waters of a lake gleamed in a fold in the undulating land. Feeling around in the bottom of her fish-bucket she said: "There's something I have to do."

She grasped the squirming, muscly little catfish and hauled him, whiskers twitching, out of the water. Pushing past her protesting mother she let herself down from the cab, clambered over a stile and hurried across a stubble field towards the lake.

"Oh!" she exclaimed suddenly when another stile in a tall hedge brought her to the bankside - the lake was beautiful, hardly a ripple disturbing its surface. Making her way to the edge of a grassy slope she dropped the catfish in with a 'plop!'. It lay there still for a moment, as if tasting the water, then unhurriedly began to explore its way forward. Soon it vanished altogether.

"I hope you have a lovely time here," Zofia said, standing. Actually, she could have spent much more time looking at the loveliness of the spot, with the rising land behind the water topped with a fine old mansion house. The whole place gave her friendly a sense of peaceful well-being. But a "parp!" from Dada's horn woke her from her reverie. Back at the truck, she found him with the bonnet up checking the engine oil; her mother was fussing around in the caravan. Clearly they were staying put for the night. Seeing her empty-handed, Dada joked: "Better tell your mother we need something else for supper tonight."

Later, she was not altogether surprised to find that the prize fish bucket now contained only eight goldfish. One squirmy black inhabitant had been removed in the nick of time.

Early next morning they were away just before first light, leaving at the same time the dairyman was cycling along the lane to milk his cows - the last time dark-eyed Zofia was this close to Brightwell. But not the last time she was reasonably close to a catfish later known as Gobblemouth.

***

14

Fast forward to the more recent events leading up to the decision to launch the Quest for the Crimson Trout.

Unusually Michael Tipton's house was empty. With his wife away he had eaten something from the freezer for supper, microwaved and unmemorable. Now the earl was looking down from his study window towards the lake, where a shortish figure was walking slowly, preoccupied. Tipton knew what was behind the man's apparently aimless wanderings: he'd seen Bryn Thomas poking around for most of the afternoon, and it could be deduced that in his fey Welsh way the archaeologist was playing hunches, following daydreams along vast timelines and trying to find landscape clues to back it all up. An odd man, a bit dozy you'd think if you didn't know him.

But Tipton had good reason to know Thomas quite well. Not all that long ago the estate had been in a fight for its very existence, threatened with compulsory purchase for housing expansion. Bryn Thomas had been called in by the developers to explore the ground ahead of starting work on new homes: a statutory obligation on the builder's part to rescue any important remains from the past which might soon be buried. But it turned out that the archaeologist's delving made building very nearly impossible while the area was searched more thoroughly. This meant Bryn had taken up more or less permanent residence in the area while the developer, losing heart, had started to look elsewhere for building land. Like a seed finding a particularly advantageous spot to germinate and grow, Bryn had stayed, and flourished - particularly since the earl had commissioned him to research the area's past stretching way past the arrival of Tipton's own ancestors, the Normans.

Like the rest of the estate, Brightwell Lake had its mysteries - not least the current and pressing problem for Tipton of a missing dog. But although that disappearance was a matter that came to the top of his mind from time to time, it was unconnected with the secrets he knew Thomas was trying to uncover. No, dammit, Bryn, not Thomas, he corrected himself - it was hard to break away from the old service

15

ways of using surnames although it did not suit modern times and he had to make a conscious effort to fit in. Old habits died hard.

Late summer colours were starting to fade with approaching dusk and a light wind ruffled the lake. It clearly brought a sudden chill, for the figure below drew his jacket more tightly about himself. He looked up at the manor house, then started to walk more briskly towards it. Tipton smiled, went to a corner cupboard and took out a bottle of whisky, put it on his desk. He set off for the kitchen for a jug of water and tumblers. To that point he'd been thinking he might have an early night. Now things looked a little more promising. He opened the front door to find Thomas already halfway across the flagstone terrace.

Framed in the doorway of his ancestral home the Earl showed some signs of his advancing age: some thinning of the hair, perhaps, more hollows in the lively face to show in relief the scar running across one eye and down his cheek - a souvenir of his bomber pilot days during the Second World War. But his frame remained upright even though stiffness in the joints was an increasing problem, especially first thing in the morning.

"Bryn - good to see you." Tipton held out a steady hand. "Come up to the study - you've time to talk? There's ham in the fridge if you want to make a sandwich to bring up too. You know where things are."

"Thanks sir. That'd be good."

Tipton winced at the old formalities reappearing: the civil 'sir' remained the Welshman's favoured way of addressing him, even though he could recollect stating 'call me Michael' on at least a dozen occasions. They both had entrenched manners, then. Tipton led him through the silent manor to the kitchen first ... of course the man hadn't eaten. He watched him cut meat, butter sliced bread, wondering why he himself hadn't chosen to eat this far better fare rather than the sad packaged meal that was already starting to give him indigestion.

16

"Mustard in that pot too. And pickled onions on the shelf, Helen's finest...this year's crop, and they're just about ready."

He could almost hear the crunch of those onions before the jar was opened.

Ever since their first meeting a strong friendship had grown between the far-from-aloof lord of the manor and the quick and inquisitive investigator of times past. Each man had a good idea of what made the other tick. Right now, Thomas had something to say, Tipton knew. He held doors open for him and soon they were sitting each side of his desk with the light outside the window now almost gone. The moon had not yet started to rise, though it was due in about an hour, a full moon at that. The Welshman ploughed steadily through his sandwich and chased it with a gulp of well-watered whiskey. Then he sat back with the smile.

"Well?" Tipton raised his eyebrows. Bryn had come here with something on his mind. But his first words were not what the Earl expected and certainly not ones he wanted to hear.

"Have they found the dog yet?"

Tipton groaned - so the bloody dog story was getting around then. A week ago a woman had been walking her pet by the lake, a small terrier, all hair and yaps, when it had chased a moorhen into the water. Of course the moorhen had done what moorhens usually do when they want to make themselves scarce, diving out of harm's way, but while the mystified dog paddled about in the reeds looking for it, there was a mighty swirl and, according to the mortified owner, a huge mouth suddenly gaped open, swallowed the dog and sank back out of sight. Unsurprisingly the owner was inconsolable. Tipton himself helped men search the reeds round the entire lake - not a trace. A giant pike perhaps? It would have to be enormous, far bigger than any of the stuffed specimens on the estate office wall.

"You've heard? We haven't found a thing - you don't know of anything that would help, I expect?"

His guest shook his head. "No. The lake's pretty deep in places. Some big fish, probably. What about pike?"

Tipton shrugged. "Your guess is as good as mine. Only thing I'm sure of is that it's not a great white shark. Dog owner's upset, as you might imagine. Seems to think it's my fault - no warnings about dangerous fish, that sort of thing. I don't know where we stand legally." He smiled. "I'm waiting for somebody to suggest we've got a crocodile problem."

Thomas laughed. "If you have, you could start a safari park, perhaps?"

Tipton topped up their drinks. Fortified, Thomas was ready to put aside the dog mystery and launch into the business that had really occupied him all afternoon. He leaned forward.

"I think I have your topography mapped pretty much from the Dark Ages forward, when the bigger landscape changes started," he said.

"Let's hear it then...if you have time, of course. And...oh, blast, I forgot, you're not going to be driving - are you? Where are you staying?"

The Welshman laughed. "The old survey cabin's just a few minutes over the fields and I often spend a couple of nights there. Carol understands so long as I call and tell her. Feel quite at home with the foxes and owls - you get used to it. No, let me sketch a couple of things out. As we've already found out this has been quite a place even before the Romans, let alone the Anglo Saxons and the Normans - your ancestors. But the signs I can see today like earthworks, walls and building remains are Dark Ages onwards, though some of the stone used was obviously recycled Roman masonry. That little stone bridge over the lake feeder stream two fields up is obviously originally Roman too. But I'm sure there's something else, something we can't see, something very, very old and in keeping with Nudd's hound and some of the other finds.

18

Missing links going right back past the Iron Age and the Bronze Age to the Neolithic, perhaps the Mesolithic too. Like I say, I can't find those links but I have a pretty good idea where they might be."

Tipton raised his eyebrows. The 'Nudd's hound' referred to was a pre-Roman artefact unearthed in the grounds, a beautiful miniature figure of a hunting dog. The hound and other ancient artefacts had been instrumental in the estate's fairly recent salvation.

"Go on."

Thomas leaned back. "How difficult would it be to drain the lake?"

For just an instant that sounded crazy to Tipton. But on a moment's reflection, and bearing in mind the fate of the luckless dog , it might not be such a bad idea. If draining the lake gave the archaeologist a chance to discover more clues to the past beneath the surface it might also show them what had happened to the unfortunate pet, thereby killing two birds with one stone. Possibly a third too, for the lake was badly silted-up in parts.

However, although the finances of the estate had become immeasurably stronger now that it was a successful healing centre, the exercise of getting the water out of the lake looked as though it might be disruptive and quite possibly hugely expensive. Also, for a time they would lose the value of having this beautiful piece of water to lift the spirits of all who came here to benefit from Brightwell's treatments, and costly and noisy machinery might have to be brought in to breech the dam, since he could no longer call on the services of old pals in 624 'Dambuster' Squadron to blast a hole in it! Surely there were other simpler methods to explore first? Divers? Expert fishermen?

"I don't suppose you know of anyone who could catch a big pike, if that's what we have?" Tipton asked Thomas.

The Welshman smiled. "No," he said. "But I think I know a man who does. Do you remember that journalist - Gerry Savage, isn't it?"

"Of course! He's a big fisherman, isn't he? I've got his number in my book. I'll phone him right away..."

Tipton was about to stand up and do just that, but Thomas was holding up one hand like a policeman stopping traffic.

"Wait. I don't expect you'd know this but old Savage hasn't been so well lately. Seems he fell down a manhole outside his own gate. Somebody had pinched the cover - they do it for the scrap metal value. Nothing really serious but he has broken one wrist and the other arm and he looks a bit like an Egyptian mummy. I think his fishing days are over ... at least for a while. All the same, he'd know just what to do, and perhaps have somebody in mind who might help. I'll go and talk with him if you like."

They agreed on that before taking one last small dram for the road, little knowing how far their discussion was going to take them.

Chapter 2

In the back of his mind, Bryn Thomas had an idea that Mike, the elder son of his partner Carol Cook and a keen angler, might well be just the person to attempt to catch Brightwell's monster, whatever it turned out to be, but Gerry Savage had an even better idea. When Thomas had outlined the project to the retired journalist, he could see Savage wanted to throw both arms in the air, but with each of them in in varying amounts of plaster all he could manage was a half-hearted gesture and a grunt of pain.

"I know Mike well. He'll help, of course he will," said Gerry, "Try to stop him ... and of course, he'd do anything for you and his Ma. But he's no pike expert, and neither am I for that matter. But listen, I know a former newspaper colleague who lives right here and he really knows his stuff so far as pike are concerned. He actually claims to have caught a British record pike. In fact, probably a European record too, maybe even the biggest in the world so far."

"And do you believe him?"

"Actually, I do. Listen, I've never heard any bull from him. *If* it is a pike, Mark Kendal will get it out."

There was a note of caution, making Bryn raise an eyebrow. "*If?*"

"Well, I've been a fisherman all my life and I've read almost everything there is to know about it, but I have never heard a real verified account of a pike swallowing a dog. But I live - just about anyway - to be corrected! And I don't think Brightwell is actually capable of producing an enormous pike - a big one perhaps, but not a monster. They only get really big in special circumstances, I understand. No, if you ask me what we're looking for is a local legend, at least with anglers at Brightwell Lake - Gobblemouth."

"Gobblemouth?"

"Gobblemouth is something nobody has actually identified, although I know of people fishing for pike who had their line smashed as if it was cotton. I don't even know who gave it the nickname, but those who claim to have seen it say it's a long but stout eel-like fish with a big wide mouth, so the title is quite apt. I'm pretty sure what you're looking for is no real mystery: it's a giant European catfish, otherwise known as a Wels, from the Danube region. But heaven only knows how it found its way here."

***

Which was almost exactly the conclusion dark-haired and tallish Mark Kendal came to when they brought him in on the round-table discussion a few days later. They were in Tipton's study grouped around the fireplace - Tipton, of course, Gerry Savage (who still looked like something from The Curse of the Mummy), the youngest of the five Mike Cook, Bryn Thomas and pike expert Kendal. Helen Tipton had left them a tray of sandwiches and a big pot of tea before heading off for a WI meeting.

"You can be sure it isn't a pike."

Kendal's tone made it clear he had no doubts that the dog-gobbler did not belong to his favourite fish species. He had told them about the campaign which had led to the capture of his big pike in Scotland, and his story gave convincing arguments for making this flat statement. Brightwell lake simply did not have a big enough food supply for a monster pike, nor would such a fish be inclined to swallow a pet dog. But after dismissing one potential culprit a smile suddenly appeared on his deeply lined and well-weathered face, and he added: "But of course I will be happy to help try and find out exactly what it is. And I do have a couple of ideas."

"You do?" said Tipton, leaning forward like the others. "Let's hear them."

Only Bryn Thomas had so far heard of Gerry Savage's 'Gobblemouth' theory, and Gerry was keeping quiet to let Kendal have his say. He found Kendal a likeable man, at times a little unpredictable but all the same a good person to have on your side. He showed he had a wide knowledge, too, particularly where natural history was concerned.

"Well, I'm ruling out alligators or crocodiles too, because I think they might have shown themselves more by now as air-breathers. Anyway, that's the least likely suggestion even though it wouldn't be beyond the realms of possibility that an overgrown pet crocodile had been released here. And before you completely dismiss the crocodile notion as fanciful, you should know that there has been an urban myth for at least 50 years that alligators lurk in the New York Sewers. Nearly everyone laughed about this but in 2008 one was fished out alive and well."

"So if it isn't a pike and it isn't a croc, what else could it be?" There was an edge of frustration in Tipton's voice. He wanted Kendal to get to the point.

"OK. I'd say either its a snapping turtle or a giant catfish. And if I was to make a choice I'd say it was the latter. There could even be more than one."

Gerry smiled - his own thoughts exactly.

"I didn't think turtles got very big," chipped in Mike Cook, who was a junior reporter on the paper which both Savage and Kendal had worked in their careers before retiring. He had grown handsomely tall and was apparently still growing in his early 20s. His confident voice showed he was not overawed in the company of these older men.

Kendal was wagging his head. "You'd be surprised. A few years back at Caldicot Castle park in Wales the groundkeepers were puzzled that all their ornamental pond's waterfowl had gradually disappeared. Nothing else was inclined to swim in it either. Finally they caught an enormous American snapping turtle. More than two feet long, it weighed 20 pounds or so and was estimated to be about

20 years old. I know that's not truly enormous as things go, but the creature has a wickedly sharp, pointed beak and a serpentine neck which it can shoot out and strike anything it fancies on the surface, then drag it under. It's formidable. The turtles aren't native to this country, and they've usually been somebody's pet before being tipped in the water because they've outgrown their tank. And outgrown their entertainment value. Think of the food bill for a turtle that's been used to eating a couple of fat ducks a week."

"Catfish can be really huge, can't they?" said Mike. He read all the fishing newspapers and magazines. He knew his stuff.

"They can," agreed Kendal. "In this country the official rod-caught record is over 60lb, and there's plenty of evidence they've been caught at least twice that size. But just minnows compared with specimens from the fish's native rivers like the Danube or the Dneiper, fish of 500, even as much as 600 pounds."

Tipton was clearly shocked at this revelation, and Bryn Thomas gave a low whistle of surprise. "*600 pounds? Really?*"

"Oh yes," said Kendal. "Big catfish of one sort or another occur all over the world - we're something of an exception having no native ones here. And in a couple of places - the Amazon, for example, and the Ganges in India - they even have a reputation as man-eaters. Closer to the truth would be that anyone who drowns from a capsize wouldn't trundle around in the river for long with these scavengers about. "

"No more splosphing in the river when I'm next on holiday, then," joked Tipton. "If we have one, and we want to catch it, what will we use for bait? Half a cow? Do people fish for them?"

"They do," said Kendal. "They have quite a following. Something as big as that makes a terrific trophy photograph, and of course they put up quite a tussle so that's a big thrill. The usual bait is a dead fish of some kind - herring, for choice, or mackerel, same as for pike. But unlike pike they tend to be mainly active at night, usually lying doggo between dawn and dusk. Surprisingly too they can be caught on quite small baits like cereal pellets soaked in fish oil - nice and smelly. They have relatively small eyes but a highly sensitive sense of smell. And those whiskers contain all sorts of sensing equipment too, so they can scent and feel for food, even detect electrical impulses from living fish, it's said. But even if you hook a big one, there's no guarantee you'll be able to land it. Not only are they strong but they have another trick up their sleeves - they can swim backwards, very strongly too."

"Are there many in this country then, considering it's not a native species?" Bryn Thomas asked.

"Quite a few," said Kendal. "And they're spreading here too, as they are in other parts of Europe where they have been introduced. Spain's River Ebro is now a recognised centre for catching big catfish and plenty of them - I'm talking of fish around 100lb or so, and the record for the river is over 250lb. But a lot of the British fish are thought to have spread from Woburn Abbey where some were put in ornamental lakes earlier last century - the lakes are connected with the River Ouse system and so they didn't stay confined for long. All Britain's big rivers are connected by some degree through the canals, and besides that people are still shoving alien species of fish where they shouldn't be. Defra has a long list of them, and it's still growing. Have a look at their rogues' gallery on the internet when you have the time. It's fascinating."

***

A plan of action started to form around the continuing discussion. Mike Cook, who judged his carp-fishing tackle ought be up to the task, and pike-expert Mark Kendal , would begin a campaign of night-fishing when time allowed them, both hoping to connect with the giant catfish. Gerry Savage pledged he would join them when he had his plaster casts taken off, but added this might not be very soon.

They were to make a start at the weekend and there was a sense of urgency about the affair because they were not only curious to see if

25

Kendal's surmise about their quarry was right, but also aware that the warm weather would not last much longer - the nights were already growing quite long and a catfish would change down into a very low gear once it became really cold.

"Let's take a punt at it," the earl said cheerily as the fireside meeting broke up. "But of course if it looks clear we aren't getting anywhere I may have to resort to Bryn's desire to drain the lake. I'm in two minds about that but there are some advantages. It'll put everyone's minds at rest to find out if there really is a giant fish there, it'll help Mr Thomas here explore bits of the past he hasn't been able to get his hands on, and it's a good chance to get some of the silt out of the lake bottom. Muck's been building up for years and the water's getting shallower and shallower."

He drew Bryn Thomas aside as they left. Mike Cook, waiting for a lift home, lingered in the doorway.

"Tell me, if we do catch this monster whatever-you-call-it, what are we going to do with it?"

Bryn shrugged.

"Exactly," said the Earl, "something of a problem, you'll agree."

When they had all gone, Tipton was not yet ready for sleep. He decided to mug up on catfish using the office computer. Siluris Glanis, he discovered, otherwise known as the Wels or European catfish, was the largest freshwater fish of the Continent. Although originally confined to eastern regions it had been spreading south and west in the last couple of centuries, largely through being introduced as a curiosity. Britain's first 'transplants' took place in the mid-1850s when the 'acclimatisation' movement was in full swing. Acclimatisation societies sprang up with the purpose of what was then thought to be a good way of enriching the fauna and flora of the world with non-native species. It's now known this was responsible for such disasters as Australia's rabbit plague.

The first acclimatisation introductions of catfish took place as far back as 1865, but it is generally thought most of the catfish in Britain are descended from specimens placed in Woburn's lakes by the Duke of Bedford in 1880. Although a water temperature of around 20 degrees - not always attained in Britain - is necessary for breeding, they have spread steadily ever since, probably as had been suggested through the drainage and navigation channels and canals linking most of the country's inland waterways.

The predatory fish-cum-scavenger was eel-like but stout, mottled, scaleless and slimy. It was easy to identify, partially because of its huge head and wide mouth but specially because of the long whiskers around the mouth which gave it and related species their name, 'catfish'. Siluris Glanis had two long 'whiskers' protruding from its upper snout, and four smaller ones dangling below. These were actually highly tuned sensors which helped it detect prey. Catfish were active hunters of other fish species and although mainly nocturnal, they could be active at dawn or dusk or even throughout dull days.

Where they were fished for with serious intent, Tipton learned, catfish had been caught on a range of baits from sprats to exotic offerings that included rats, chickens and even whole rabbits. Why anybody would want to catch one was a mystery to non-angler Tipton: apparently they did not make good eating.

"You sound like quite a character," he observed before he closed down his computer. It was not without a twinge of conscience concerning the recent fate of someone's adored pet.

The study clock showed that more than an hour and a half had slipped past since his last guest left. Suddenly he felt really, really tired.

Chapter 3

Bryn Thomas' affection for Mike's mother Carol had grown steadily. They first met when Mike discovered the 'treasure' that saved the Brightwell estate from a development - a little stone dog that marked the lakeside as an ancient site. They now lived happily together. However, she was not upset to let Bryn spend some of his working nights in the old portable cabin that had been used for his rescue archaeology survey of the fields round Brightwell Lake during the 'dark ages' (Tipton's term) when it had been threatened with a compulsory purchase order. Bryn was still studying some of the finds that had helped to stave off this threat and it sometimes meant him staying late at the cabin, which he had made comfortable enough for overnighting. Now, however, because it was so close to the lake, the cabin was a handy HQ for fishermen during the campaign to catch the Brightwell dog-snacker.

Kendal and Mike spearheaded this effort, but both had recruited other fishermen they knew to join in. Tipton sportingly put a bounty of £50 on the target's head - metaphorically speaking, for all were under strict instructions to keep the fish alive - and consequently the two leaders were never short of assistance. At times as many as ten bounty-hunters were spaced round the lake. The camaraderie among members of this modern-day 'posse' was infectious and at least at first everyone's spirits - and optimism - stayed high. Tipton's other contribution to the campaign - and a very popular contribution it turned out to be - was a nightly delivery of hot pizzas and canned drinks to the bivouac encampments. The night-time lakeside banter was rich - it was a good job none of Tipton's clients at the sanatorium ever strayed near the water after dark.

Kendal, who lived alone in the nearby village, took on the majority of the 'night shift' supervision responsibilities and slept in the cabin by day.

Since they very often shared the same small bay to set up their tackle twenty or so yards apart, a close friendship grew up between the Kendle and Mike Cook during the all-too-brief time that was spent spent trying to catch the elusive monster. Mike sensed there was a lot to learn from the man's obvious expertise, and his tales of fishing exploits always had a tinge of high adventure.

The assault itself was not short of excitement, although the lengthening nights with cooling temperatures made the chance of catching any catfish (let alone a big one) more and more unlikely. But in the main the fruitless spells were enlivened for around an hour after setting up in the dusk, and then again for an hour around dawn, when small jack-pike made concerted attacks on their herring and mackerel baits. And then one morning Kendal struck into something really big and called Mike over.

"Do you think it's Gobblemouth?" the young man was excited.

Kendal was fishing his baits a fairly long way out, and like Mike he had two rods set up.

"Hard to say at this range," said Kendal leaning back to put some pressure on his fish, and earning a sizeable kick in return. "But I think you'd better pull in that other line for me, if you don't mind - just in case."

The light was growing as Mike picked up the redundant rod and started to reel the line in. They could see some massive swirls way out in the water. Then they both said "Ah!" in unison as a long snout followed by a gold-green body emerged from the water and shook violently to try to loose the hook-hold. Shouts of encouragement came from the other fishermen camped around the bank, carrying clearly across the water.

"Pike," Kendal said in a hushed voice, "And a good one."

A quarter of an hour later Mike obligingly extended Kendal's big landing net in the water so that the big fish could be drawn over it and lifted out safely. Kendal was able to tease out the hook while the

29

fish still lay in the net, but before putting it back he rummaged for his spring balance and briefly hoisted fish, net and all into the air for a reading.

"Twenty-eight pounds I reckon, allowing for the weight of the net. What a beauty - I think we're possibly looking at the biggest pike in Brightwell."

Mike nodded in agreement. "But it's not a catfish, is it?"

"That's for sure," Kendal said as they watched the pike swim away free into the lake.

Later that week, after two nights of hard frosts and many more smaller pike, they consulted all the other campaigners and then went to Tipton and admitted defeat.

"Dash it - does that mean we'll have to wait for spring?" the earl said.

"It would be best," said Kendal. "But if you ask me, I don't think we're getting anywhere with fishing. Perhaps our friend Gobblemouth is more interested in eating ducks, like the Caldicot turtle."

"You mean I should go ahead and drain the lake - Bryn Thomas's original plan?"

"It's beginning to look like that."

***

It was the following April before everything was ready to begin draining Brightwell Lake. Through the winter, Tipton had been racking his brain to remember if his father had ever said anything about a drain or plug hole that would make getting the water out of the lake easier. Nothing came to mind, and finally, almost in desperation, called on an old Air Force pal, now a retired water-engineer, to see if he could help. They walked round the lake and stopped by the dam end, it's deepest part, on a raw January day.

"What I'm looking for is a pipe just under the surface, or rather the mouth of one," Brian Wright said. "If they were any good at making a lake in the first place they would have put one in, a sort of automatic levelling device in addition to the dam overspill. It would be as good as having a plug because we might be able to chop it off at the bottom. And then bingo, all the water would run out. It would either be tight under this bank somewhere, though it could perhaps be a bit further out in the lake. But then again it could be under our feet. I suppose the stream makes sure the water level is always topped up, or the pipe would show up now and then."

"There's a spring under the lake as well, I believe," said Tipton. "The level has stayed bang on where it is for as long as I can remember."

Continuing along the dam wall, former flight engineer Wright, now silver-haired with a shiny bald red island in the middle of his head, nearly tripped on the edge of a large flagstone set in the bank.

"What's this?" he said, kneeling down to pull grass and weeds away from one of its edges.

"I don't know - I haven't really noticed it before. But I'm pretty sure it was always there. Is that what we're looking for?"

"Could be," said Wright. "Here, grab this edge and we'll lift...one, two, three..."

They revealed a brick-lined water-filled cavity with a short culvert leading to the lake. Right in the middle and just under the surface was the mouth of a six-inch diameter iron pipe. Water was continually slopping over its edge and disappearing.

"Ah hah!" Wright exclaimed, "Even better!"

"What?"

In spite of the coldness of the day the man took off his jacket, knelt down and, rolling up the sleeves of his shirt and jumper, plunged his arm into the icy water beside the central pipe and groped around.

31

Grasping something he held it up for Tipton to see. It was the end of a chain.

"Your ancestors were pretty good at foreseeing situations just like this," he said. "All in all it's quite a complicated piece of hydraulics. I can virtually guarantee that if we haul on this we'll pull out the plug together with the other end of the pipe and the bath water will run away. Eureka, as Pythagoras might have said ... or was it Archimedes?"

***

Remembering that long ago his gamekeeper had advised thinning out of the lake's coarse fish, Tipton had promised again to give most of the fish he did not want to a number of local fishing clubs to stock their own waters. He'd had to call in the Environment Agency to make sure everything complied with fish-movement rules, and the fisheries advisor they sent round was a valuable help on many fronts. Among his suggestions was the hire of three large above-ground splash pools with aerators to hold any fish which would eventually be returned to the lake. He had also introduced Tipton to a very interesting man indeed: Roger Percy, who not only owned a fish smokery business but was an expert at transporting live fish.

"You take elvers as far as *Spain*?" Tipton said with incredulity when the casually-dressed businessman told him about his business. That was a revelation.

"Well, actually, we even take them to Japan," said Percy. "But not in the truck, of course - I have part share in a small aircraft for that."

Percy had agreed to distribute Brightwell's 'spare' fish to other local waters during a slack couple of days in a very busy spring period, landing his lorry and drivers 'just to stop the lads from getting idle'. Tipton had been amazed that any notion of a charge, apart from diesel costs, was waived.

"I like to do my bit for the community," said Percy. "Besides, you're one of my best customers for our smoked salmon."

32

"We are?" It was news to Tipton, although he did know smoked salmon was always a popular item on the menu at the sanatorium.

***

Throughout the intervening winter Tipton had also been thinking long and hard about what he might do with a giant catfish that he definitely did not want to go back in the lake - especially a catfish with a taste for small and possibly quite expensive pet dogs, let alone all the water's wildfowl.

He was not altogether surprised to find that the Environment Agency was very concerned about allowing such monsters as Gobblemouth to spread and had strict rules forbidding their movement to a water which did not already contain the species. Further research on the internet led him to a society that helped to 'rehome' catfish (so Tipton's problem wasn't as unique as he'd first imagined it to be). He also learned, however, that some of the waters with a reputation for catfish-angling were very heavily fished and regularly restocked so that catching one could be virtually guaranteed. Something in him wondered if this was strictly fair, though he was prepared to acknowledge that his ideas of sporting fairness could be a little past their sell-by date. Brightwell, on the other hand, was run as a 'natural' fishery that he'd never had to restock - and in any event it could hardly be described as over-fished.

He put all this at the back of his mind while the lake was being drained.

As predicted by his engineer friend Brian Wright, who came along for the occasion, after a spell of rocking the drain-pipe while somebody hauled on the chain, something gave. An 18ft metal pipe was hoisted through years of layered silt to reveal the club-like 'plug' at its bottom end.

"Just wood and greasy leather with a bit of pitch," Wright grinned. "Preserved all this time - quite remarkable. We could almost put it back as it was and it would go on doing the job for another couple of hundred years. The pipe's corroded but the metal's thick and it'll probably last forever."

A low gurgle was coming from the direction of the lake's overspill sluice and Tipton, Wright and a little group of spectators went over to investigate. Low down on one of the stream's banks a jet of filthy black water was pouring out of another pipe that had been unnoticed for years. The lake had begun to empty without having to resort to bouncing bombs!

But alas, the optimism brought by the disappearing water didn't last long. Two days later, to everyone's dismay, the level of the lake had dropped a mere two feet overall, where it stopped obstinately. Tipton called Brian Wright to break the bad news.

"Ah, I suspected that might happen," he said. "It means the stream is putting in as much water as the pipe is taking out, perhaps even more. I don't think they diverted the original watercourse to fill the lake in the first place, so there must be a by-pass channel they made to run it round the outside. You'll have to go upstream of the lake to find where it starts. You're looking for another culvert or perhaps an open ditch that skirts the entire lake. And there'll be some method of stopping the stream to drive it into the channel - guides to drop planks in, or a big flagstone that lifts upright against some stonework in the banks. If it's an open ditch you might need to get it cleared out before youblock the main flow."

Archaeologist Bryn Thomas had of course surveyed the whole are and was able to point out accurately where the channel ran. Tipton had to stand down an army of fishermen while they cleaned out a clearly-defined ditch that looped round the wooded side of the lake. New planks had to be shaped to fit the iron stanchions that would divert the stream. Once the planks were dropped in place and the flow was shifted to its new course, it all worked a treat, and once again the water level in the lake started to fall. It was painfully slow, however, and Tipton was reminded again that it was believed there was also a spring at the bottom of the lake. Exactly where that was he had never been told, even if his father had known.

It took another week before they could make a proper start. In a muddy 3ft deep lagoon left against the dam end of the lake, the bulk of the fish were marshalled towards a strong net supplied by the Environment Agency, two men holding upright poles at each end and ready to come together once the purse-end of the arrangement was full. Large fish were being scooped out individually by helping anglers armed with big landing nets, and hurried to the waiting tanks.

There were plenty of specimen size, including the big pike Kendal had caught in the previous autumn (she had shed a few pounds in spawning, a recent occurrence). However both Mike Cook and Gerry Savage were disappointed that the biggest carp was a mere 20lb. Somehow a very large carp nicknamed 'Brassribs' had perished in the seven years since Mike Cook had caught it, a feat witnessed by Gerry. But even more disappointing for all of them was the non-appearance - so far at any rate - of a large catfish. Any catfish at all for that matter.

Apart from that, the whole operation went fairly well. Roger Percy's fish transporter truck, which for this occasion was fitted with just three large aerated plastic tanks (it could be fitted with up to eight of these, paired in tandem along the truck bed and secured in place with stout tethers) turned up to take the unwanted fish from three weighty sweeps of the net once the catches were sorted into 'keepers' and 'goers'.

The effort to clear out the lake bed started once the fish had gone. In places there was a layer of three to four feet of black and smelly silt, tons and tons of it, the notable exception being a clean water puddle about ten feet across right at the middle. From this a little rivulet of similarly clean water trickled towards the drain-hole at the dam end: this was Brightwell's spring, and undoubtedly, Tipton was sure, the feature from which the lake originally got its name.

In the exposed bed of the lake a small yellow caterpillar-tracked bulldozer was tasked with methodically shoving swathes of silt to a gradually sloping gravel bank where a JCB waited to scoop up bucketfuls and load it straight into muck-spreaders sent from local farms, waiting in a queue to cart the valuable organic fertilizer away. The bulldozer-driver was under strict instructions to shovel-up soft material only and avoid digging the blade into the old clay bed of the lake. He was adhering diligently to this advice while his swipes brought him closer and closer to the edge of the spring when, out of the blue, the black goo just in front of the blade moved. Astonished, the driver stopped his machine abruptly, switched the engine into idle, and walked along one of the half-submerged tracks to investigate. Wallowing in the semi-liquid mud he first made out a gaping mouth fringed with long, twitching whiskers. Then behind this, small but at least a foot apart, he saw looking up at him two small, glittering, dark and (he thought) malevolent eyes.

"Here," he reported to Kendal on his mobile phone when he got back to his seat. "You'll never guess what I've just found."

***

What he had found, of course, was Gobblemouth, who by this time was a mighty large fish, not to say magnificent in catfish terms.

Hatched in a lair scraped in an underhang of the Danube's bank, he and his siblings were at first little more than wriggling black embryos hardly distinguishable from tadpoles save for a single small barbel at the business end. The whole brood was guarded by their father, a truly enormous male catfish, mum (like all her kind) having lost interest in the proceedings after laying her eggs. Anything with the inclination to eat a small catfish or two, or even looking at them for that matter, was quickly driven away or eaten by dad. His parental role lasted while they remained helpless, surviving on a tiny yolk sac. But they grew quickly, and by the time Gobblemouth had been rudely snatched out of his home river by a beautiful gypsy girl, their

36

guardian father too had stopped caring about what was to become of them.

After his capture, the infant fish that was to become known as Gobblemouth didn't particularly like being driven round in a slopping bucket of water, but being fed on a regular and ample supply of chopped up earthworms (later even live goldfish) helped him to become resigned to the situation. Then, quite suddenly, all of that came to an end. He was dropped into an altogether more comfortable billet, a large stillwater lake crammed with every kind of aquatic life imaginable. More than he could possibly eat in one go!

Shallows and deeps, areas of weed, clean gravel and black mud were all welcome parts of the new home, but one of its two major disadvantages became clear as he explored and grew: the winters were often cold and unfailingly very long. Actually, what he really noticed was that the warm sunny times were quite short, and all to soon he had to think about digging himself into one of a series of lairs he had built to snuggle into and sleep off the winters.

The other major disadvantage of this otherwise lovely billet was that the water held no other catfish, in particular no female catfish, which meant that once a year when his thoughts turned to fatherhood - an unbidden time of restlessness and fruitless searching - there was nothing for it but to endure until the feeling passed away.

Otherwise, things were great. It hadn't been long before he'd actually outgrown anything that might have wanted to eat him, even one very large pike. Waking at dusk every spring, summer and autumn morning, he patrolled the margins of the lake until the sun once more started to climb in the sky. Woe betide any snoozing fish whose presence was picked up by his acute senses of smell and taste concentrated around his nostrils and along the whip-like barbels, or tentacles, that had developed where once there had been only one - two long ones on his broad forward snout and four shorter ones on his chin.

He found the ideal spot for his master-lair one late autumn day when there had actually been a nip of frost overnight. Until that point he'd had a variety of resting places, usually choosing spots where the black ooze was deepest so that he could wriggle most of his body undercover and keep it well away from the ice that sometimes roofed his world. But straying to the middle of the lake on this particular day - not among his normal hunting grounds - he found a shallow depression amid the ooze that was anything but black. In fact, it was nearly white, and investigating further he discovered a bed of fine silvery sand agitated from below by clear, fresh water billowing upwards. At this time of the year the lake in general was becoming stale from the heat of the summer and the de-oxygenating effect of layers of rotting leaves, but by contrast the spring that he had just found had plenty of oxygen in it, invigoratingly so, and its temperature was perhaps a degree or so above the water in the rapidly-cooling lake.

Always the opportunist, the big catfish found this warmer location meant could put off hibernation for at least a month longer than would normally be the case, and he was not alone because other fish were also happier here. But bit by bit, however, they learned he was a 'companion' they could not trust, at least until he scooped himself a hollow and backed into it to start his long sleep. Irritatingly, however, there was a hard object in this nest which kept tumbling back down into the bottom whenever he pushed it out. In the end, too tired and cold to bother with it any longer, he moulded his body around it and abandoned himself to the worst the winter could bring. Come spring, when he at last emerged from these quarters, he was too hungry to bother making his bed, and in the following winter when he retreated there again the hitherto annoying lump had become a familiar piece of furniture.

In the summer that followed and for many summers afterwards, the catfish developed a taste for water birds as well as fish that inhabited the lake's weedy margins, and it was in these regions he spent most of his time, retreating on bright days to one of four summer refuges chosen for their comfort and ability to supply a ready meal whenever he started stalking.

Young birds, he found, were particularly easy to catch, mostly following their mothers in long strings. They were not, however, very substantial meals for the large bulk he was now attaining. It wasn't long before he graduated to adult moorhens and coots which either obligingly dived down into his domain or dangled their legs enticingly through the surface. His first mallard, which he caught snoozing unawares with its head under its wing, was far more satisfying. Once his formidable gastric juices had set to work on feathers, bones and gristle, it was less of a challenge to his digestion than he might have imagined it to be.

Aware he could eat almost anything so long as he could get it into his wide mouth, there was now no stopping him...

Chapter 4

The moment young Mike Cook uttered the fateful words "frying fish" Tipton shuddered, for there was indeed this distinctive smell hanging in the air in what now seemed a God-forsaken spot in the middle of France. In his mind he saw the huge fish that he and his companions had taken such care over being hacked into cutlets and grilled, then passed around to eager diners.

The gendarmes meanwhile were also sniffing the air and talking excitedly among themselves. Kendal, whose French wasn't all that bad, went over to them.

"They're saying the smell is coming from the direction of the municipal campsite down by the river," he reported back. "They're going down to investigate. Do we want to come along?"

They followed a little black Peugeot crammed with policemen through the village backstreets. While they were still travelling downwards towards the river an ear-splitting wail struck up - the gendarmes had switched on their siren as well as a flashing blue light on top of the vehicle. Tipton groaned.

"That isn't going to help matters much," he observed drily. "Haven't they ever heard of the element of surprise?"

At the ungated entrance to the site the gendarmes switched of the bellowing alarm, pulled up beside the road, grouped, and went in on foot, moving cautiously even though, as Tipton had observed, they were hardly unannounced. One even pulled his pistol out of its holster until a frown from his superior made him put it back: fish-stealing was hardly a capital offence, and there was little chance they would come under fire. It was dark and moonless, and as it was late the campsite lights were out. Tipton, Kendal and Mike Cook followed a little distance behind, trying to keep on the grass verges and avoid making giveaway noises on gravel.

At first they heard voices towards the centre of the park, which was dotted with caravans set amid low shrubs. But then came a low double whistle, and all fell silent. Lights in most of the vans went out. The policemen and Tipton's group stopped momentarily and Tipton had the sensation that figures were moving around them in the dark; the creak of a couple of caravan doors and clicks of locks confirmed this. Stealthily, they all moved on, only to stop again beside the park's ablutions block. He wasn't at all surprised to find the policemen grouped around the scene of what had obviously been a jolly little barbecue, the boulder-ringed fire recently put out but still smouldering. Nearby, an unlidded 'poubelle' was overflowing with empty supermarket wine cartons and the unmistakable remains of three large rainbow trout...

***

It is impossible to know if Gobblemouth linked the low warning whistle with an event from his distant past, but in one of tanks of the transporter parked at the remote end of the site he certainly heard the gendarmes clambering up on the truck bed and soon afterwards peering into the containers with the aid of flashlights. Tipton, Kendal and Mike Cook, who followed the policemen and made a quick inspection of the tank contents, were mighty relieved to find him intact. In fact, apart from the loss of a few of the bigger trout, no further damage had been done.

The gendarmes, of course, were busily knocking on doors and enquiring what had been going on and how the English fish-transporter had found its way to the park. Tipton could see from his perch on the truck bed that they were getting no more than baffled shrugs and feigned innocence for their efforts. Nobody knew anything at all, it was a complete mystery, *"everyone has been asleep for ages,"" why don't you try the caravan next door..."*

But Tipton's relief that the mission was back on track was short lived for, letting go of the side of the tank in order to lower himself to the ground, he missed his footing and fell heavily, cracking his

41

head sharply on the rim of the truck's rear outer wheel at the same time. The last thought crossing his mind before he blacked out was the ugly and angry wide-eyed head of Gobblemouth as he had first seen it in the mud of Brightwell Lake.

***

They had called Tipton down from the house as soon as the bulldozer driver found the big fish. He sent the JCB with its wide bucket out to scoop him up, water, mud and all. Mark Kendal and Gerry Savage, who had been supervising the fish-rescues during the draining of the lake, were on hand with a net sling and scales to weigh the monster - at 56lb it was below the unofficial 62lb British rod-caught record but nevertheless a whopper. But causing just as much stir was the object found in the mud that Gobblemouth had been dredged up with - a three-inch high finely-worked gold figurine of a kneeling girl.

"It's almost as if the fish had been guarding it," Tipton told Bryn Thomas after calling him up to the house "to see something pretty amazing."

The stunned and delighted archaeologist whistled when he saw it. Tipton passed it to him and he turned it over and over.

"Your were certainly right about the 'pretty'," he said.

"Well - is it very old?" said Tipton.

"I'd say."

Bryn took it away for further study, which left Tipton with the problem of what to do with the big catfish. Still he hadn't been able to make a decision on his dilemma, other than that he was determined the fish would not be killed. But in two weeks, once it was refilled, the lake would be restocked with a lot of its original fish and the above-ground plunge pools that he had hired to hold them for the draining operation would have to go back whence they came.

At this point there was another fortuitous surprise for Tipton: the enthusiastic young woman chemist loaned by the Environment Agency to keep a check on water quality throughout the operation informed him he was sitting on a valuable source of mineral water - the very stuff that fed the spring. On further analysis, it was found it probably had too high a sulphur content to be sold as table water, but it was entirely suitable as a spa drink, taken in small quantities.

"Like taking the waters at Bath?" he said to the chemist.

"Almost exactly," was the reply. "Constant temperature, same sort of minerals, perhaps with a few extras, but far, far more dilute and less radioactive. But maybe just as unpleasant, depending on your taste of course."

"Radioactive!"

The chemist laughed at his alarm and patted him on the shoulder. "Not to worry - tiny, tiny quantities. Not enough to do anyone any harm. If you want a pure supply, it'll mean a borehole down to the aquifer away from the lake. Should pop up under pressure, like an artesian spring. I know outfits that will do this for you, if you like? Should fit in nicely with the kind of business you're running here."

Delighted, Tipton put the plan in motion.

A few days later, fresh stream water was pouring back into the lake and its level was gradually rising. Soon there was enough depth for some of the fish to go back. Kendal and Savage were in charge again, and Tipton found them looking into the container that held the bigger fish, including Gobblemouth.

"Ah yes," he said, looking at the skulking monster in the bottom of the tank. "I still don't know what to do with that beastie. I think my Micawberish attitude is beginning to desert me. Any ideas?"

They hadn't. But Kendal mentioned the catfish-rehoming organisation that Tipton had already considered.

"It's a possibility. But there's something stopping me. I don't quite know what it is, but I think it's the feeling I could be taking him out of the frying pan and throwing him into the fire," said Tipton. "I can't question the motives of the people running the scheme - I'm pretty sure they have the best interests of the fish at heart. But all the same if he goes into a recognised catfish lake, with dozens of people after his hide day and night, he'd never have the peace he's enjoyed at Brightwell. Do you know what I mean? It doesn't seem fair somehow."

Kendal frowned. "I sort of see what you're getting at," he said, "but anglers are pretty careful with their catches these days, you know. Bad handling is poor sportsmanship."

Tipton nodded. "All the same, I can't help feeling there's something better. But I'm blowed if I know what it is. In the meantime, do you think he'd accept the Home Farm pond as an alternative residence? Temporary, of course. If nothing else comes up, I'll go down the rehoming route."

He took them to see the pond. In the centre of a large quadrangle of animal sheds, it was a gem among animal watering-holes, built further ago than anyone alive remembered. Stout stone walls with interconnecting gates divided the quadrangle's space into four separate yards, and the walls continued on into the water and met in the middle. Low down and out of sight there were six-inch diameter connecting pipes between the four sections, so the water-level in each always matched that of the others. The cattle, sheep or pigs placed in each of the yards could always be kept separate, even if the cows went belly-deep in the spring-fed water to cool off on warm days. And it was, of course, beloved of ducks and geese, many of which were in the water during the inspection.

"He wouldn't have the run of all of the sections - couldn't get through the pipes," Tipton said, adding anxiously: "Do you think it'll do? It's the best I can think of for now."

Gerry Savage made them all laugh.

"Have you asked the ducks?"

"I have actually thought about what to fed him with and a solution has come up," said Tipton. "I've had a very kind offer from Roger Percy - the fish transporter man, you know? I told him my problem and he's going to let me collect fish-frames and heads from his smokery that would normally go out for composting. Recycling - very politically correct!"

"Fish frames?" said Kendal, puzzled.

"Fishmonger-speak for fish bones."

"That's ideal," said Gerry. "But as you say, it's not forever, is it? Might not be exactly cruel to hold him here as a pet, but I've a feeling you wouldn't like that to go on for too long, would you? For his sake, of course."

"Of course not. Like I said, I'm sure there's a solution."

***

There was. It came out of the blue from Roger Percy when he called round to pick up a couple of fish transporter tanks left by the lakeside, and the conversation once more lighted on Tipton's dilemma of what to do with Gobblemouth.

"I don't suppose you've thought of taking him back where he came from, have you?"

Chapter 5

At these words a thrill ran through Tipton's body. It defied his advancing age, and for a moment carried him back to the pre-sortie night chill with his big bomber's engines warming up ready to tow a glider full of troops to the front. Surprised and off guard, he heard himself saying: "What a bloody brilliant idea!"

But the momentary surge in his spirits was tempered by a following thought that such a mission could not possibly be fulfilled. His shoulders sank. Perhaps the man was just joking?

"Do you mean it? But how?"

Percy grinned, raising a roguish eyebrow.

"I've got the means if you've got the commitment."

***

"Honestly, Giles, I know this is madness but I tell you I haven't felt so positive for years."

Tipton was talking to his much younger brother.

"Trouble is, it will cost us a bit too. You don't think I'm being completely irresponsible?"

"Not so long as you take me along to keep an eye on you. You can't dangle an adventure like that in front of my eyes and expect me to stay at home."

***

The plan Tipton had then hatched with Roger Percy had not been too complicated in itself but the path to its achievement was lined with regulations and it would take some time to bring everything together.

"Once the elver run is over and everyone's got their fish, I turn the truck over to charters for shifting other kinds of fish around, mainly trout," Roger Percy explained.

Tipton had already been amazed by the extent of Percy's business: the man not only owned the smokery but supplied a lot of first class restaurants with all kinds of fish throughout the country and beyond. His exporting enterprises included flying live elvers as far as Japan and other Asian countries. Nearer, the fish-transporter that he helped out with at the draining of Brightwell made forays deep into Europe to supply the little 'glass eels' to fish farms which would grow them on.

Trout, too, made the journey overseas, particularly useful breeding strains and young stock fish. And rather than running back with empty tanks, he could often bring live fish back to this country, especially uncommon strains of whitefish, trout and char, which restaurants were eager to have because of their novel table appeal.

"A trout is a trout, surely?" Tipton said at this revelation.

"You can be forgiven for thinking that," said Percy. "But even here in this country the trout of one river or lake can be completely different in appearance and even in the colour of their flesh from one another. Why, I can show you two lochs up in Sutherland with so-called brown trout with orange scales and bright pink meat in one of them, and lovely silvery little fish with perfectly white meat in the other, yet the lakes are scarcely a mile apart. Both the same species but completely different in many respects. Evolution in progress, I suppose you have to call it. Char and whitefish - a sort of freshwater herring - also have distinctive strains peculiar to certain lakes. But that's my ulterior motive for helping you out with your catfish pal."

"It is?"

"Yes. Crimson trout."

"*Crimson trout*?"

Percy gave him another of his roguish looks, and just for a moment Tipton saw behind this the flash of an astute business mind.

"Don't look so puzzled. And look, I would have helped you out anyway without an ulterior motive. When the idea of running the big fish back to Europe came to me it seemed too big an adventure to miss out on, even if I have to enjoy it vicariously. I immediately thought of the River Ebro - you've heard of that?"

"It's a name that came up when I looked-up some details on the internet," said Tipton. "It's full of rather big catfish, isn't it?"

"Yes. There's not much I don't get to hear about where fish and fishing are concerned, and the Ebro would have fitted in nicely with delivering some hatchling arctic char to Spain - do you see where I'm coming from? Only I'm afraid the Ebro might not be the place your catfish actually came from - though who's to know, eh? No - catfish like yours are native to the waters well to the north west of Spain, into the Balkans: the Danube system. And when I thought of that area, crimson trout also clicked into place."

Roger Percy seemed to be enjoying spinning things out, Tipton thought; he was also wondering again whether he was really listening to a credible plan or a bit of nonsense, albeit nonsense that delighted him. He decided to hear the man out.

"I first heard of crimson trout back in the 1990s," Percy said. "One of the men who came to work in the packing department told me about them. He'd been a soldier, part of a peacekeeping force, posted in one of the mountain valleys in what the newspapers and television nowadays call 'the former Yugoslavia'. One day he and his pals went into some remote bar and had supper there. They were served this astonishing fish, redder on the outside than a goldfish and just as bright if not brighter inside - crimson, he said. Tasty too. And it was lightly speckled - but unmistakably some kind of trout. I don't know if you've noticed or not but I get quite excited about fish. I showed him pictures of different kinds of trout and char, but all he could say was they were 'much, much redder'. And they'd asked the proprietor where the fish came from he just said 'the little lake up the road' pointing up the mountain.

"Of course, they had other things on their mind and weren't curious enough to find out where that might be. After a while I forgot about it too ... until a year ago, when I heard the same tale from one of my customers who had actually been on holiday to the region. Different restaurant, perhaps, but same region, same kind of fish. They're not very big, five or so inches, and they serve three or four of them on a plate, grilled fresh, for a meal. It has intrigued me ever since. Do you know, I even dream about them sometimes."

He laughed.

"You probably think I'm crazy, but I have to find them. I have to get some."

"So you've never seen one?"

"Never."

"And you'd go all that way just to try to find some little fish you've never even seen?"

Another laugh.

"You *do* think I'm crazy! Look, of course It's not as daft as it seems - you don't get this far in business by being dippy. And I wouldn't even think of despatching a 20-tonne fish transporter to that area without piggy-backing it on a commercial venture. Do you know how many miles to a gallon that thing does? It's more a question of how many gallons to the mile. No, I've still got a head on my shoulders - and it happens there's just the right opportunity coming up. Now, vis a vis your catfish, are you up for it too?"

***

It was crazy. And quite complicated. But it succeeded in restoring Tipton's spirit of adventure, something that had been missing from his life for some time ... and it could just work.

The plan they drew up (raising occasional anxious frowns from Helen Tipton) went like this: In the latter part of September, Percy's tanker would be loaded up with the char fry for Spain and some breeding-size trout for a fish-farmer friend in Southern France, right up against the Pyrenees. There was also trailer room for another tank which would be assigned to Gobblemouth, who could not be trusted to ride safely with other fish. There would be stopovers on the way down through France to the first delivery point, with suitable places picked in advance, one in a secure lorry park and the second at a farmyard booked through one of Percy's agents in the area. This second site was beside a trout stream running off the Massif Centrale and it offered them the chance to give all the fish a change of water should that be necessary (the tanker truck carried tanks of oxygen to aerate the water whenever that was needed: the water quality was monitored constantly). The site was also near a village where the expedition members could eat that night.

When they continued on from this point (so the plan went) and reached the French fish farm they would offload the breeding stock and also transfer the fingerlings to a fish-transporter sent up from Spain by the farm that had bought them. That left the lorry empty apart from Gobblemouth, but the newly-vacated space had been booked for eating-size live rainbows to be picked up at two more fish farms between the Pyrenees and the French/Italian border for the onward three-day journey towards the land of the crimson trout. Here, Percy hoped, he would not only have the lake finally pinpointed but also fishermen waiting with a live catch of crimson trout to send back to England. If that second bit did not materialise, there would be rod-fishermen in the working party who might be able to catch enough of the fish to make the venture just viable. And somewhere within this outward journey, they would be close enough to the Danube, or one of its main tributaries, to return Gobblemouth to his original home.

Once this was all accomplished, the return journey with the crimson trout (if any) would also see multiple pick-ups of brown and rainbow trout from France for the ever-hungry London restaurant market, plus some lobsters and a couple of sacks of live oysters from Brittany. Going back home, just as much care would have to be exercised to keep all the fish in good health, although there would be no need for Tipton and his part of the crew to attend the later proceedings, of course.

The Percy fish-transporter was a leading example of its kind. Extremely adaptable, it could be fitted with a variety of combinations of plastic tanks of varying sizes but more often than not with four on each side of the truck bed so that they were paired along its length. At the tractor end and up against the driving cab, a large fibreglass cabin held the bottled oxygen and pumps to aerate the tanks and keep the fish healthy, and there was also a heating and refrigerator unit with its own circulation system to keep the water warm or cool depending on conditions. The cabin was also a locker for tarpaulins so that the tanks could be sheeted when required. It held too a large rolled-up net and long handled nets for dipping out individual fish and whisking them quickly from tank to the river, pond or lake that was to be their new home. Fish could also be delivered in bulk by opening a hatch at the bottom of each tank to send them speedily down a chute with minimal handling. There was also a built-in fold-up stepladder to make it easy for people to get on the truck bed.

The date they picked for the expedition's departure was September 20, when most European national holidays were over and traffic (and consequent costs in terms of delays) would hopefully be lighter.

While Tipton's wife Helen worried about any medical emergencies that might arise, particularly so far as her husband was concerned, she would never have dreamed of stopping him from going. The retreat and sanatorium business was ably run by Giles' son (another Mark in addition to Kendal) who hardly needed much assistance. At least Giles was going along with the trip to help his older brother. Gerry Savage, unfortunately, was still recuperating too slowly from his accident to be a part of the group. He didn't want to be a burden. But he had no great problem with that, agreeing to help out with any diplomacy at home if anything went amiss. Mark Kendal would have gone under his own steam if there had been no place for him, and would be taking his campervan along (he had just treated himself to a new model). It would not only house him and Mike but would also serve as a mobile canteen for everybody else. And an extra fridge had been fitted to carry frozen packs of herring for feeding Gobblemouth. Mike Cook, who was rapidly losing his youthful gangliness and was keen on rugby as well as fishing, was given temporary leave from his newspaper to accompany the party so long as he sent back reports of their progress and provided a fuller feature article on their return.

Roger Percy was simply unable to join in the adventure because of pressure of work, although he clearly wished it was otherwise. Instead, he was sending a young employee, Vicky Price, to look after the considerable amount of paperwork needed along the way - transporting fish across an entire continent was a complicated business. Vicky, blonde, bright and petite, quickly built up a bulging briefcase of essential papers. And Roger also provided a driver, Derek Jones. He was temporarily without a co-driver with the necessary licensing, so a temporary post was advertised locally "although I'd rather have someone I know and trust". But Derek was a local man, and in spite of an inclination to look on the black side of things he was strong, clear-headed and totally reliable. This meant whoever they hired would be well supervised. As they neared the start date, however, Pedro DeAvila was the one and only only applicant.

Roger Percy was providing the lion's share of the costs. This included accommodation for Vicky Price and, turn and turn about, for the drivers: Jones and DeAvila would alternately sleep in the overnight compartment space behind their seats in the lorry cab both as a security measure and as duty oxygenator operators should the water quality deteriorate.

Tipton and Giles were taking Vicky along in their comfortable Range Rover; her hotel costs were also being paid by the smokery proprietor.

A day before departure, Gobblemouth was netted - somewhat docilely as it turned out - from the farm pond, and as he was reckoned to be tough enough to stand handling more than the fragile smaller trout, he was the first of the fish to be placed in a container that would confine him for the coming days of travel. His plastic tank had been created at no little expense by Roger Percy from a large green plastic container previously used to carry sea-water. It took up the space of two of the twinned trout containers at the back of the truck, almost reaching each side of the truck's bed, and Roger had supervised its construction back at the works of the manufacturer who made it originally. He had insisted on adding a locking cover for the tank-bottom drainage cock so that it would not be accidentally knocked off, and the top entrance had been enlarged from a two-foot diameter round hole to a three foot by three foot square hole with a translucent watertight lid. Once secured on the transporter, water circulation and oxygenation pipes were plumbed in, together with a temperature sensor. Lifted by four people in a rubberised canvas sling which Kendal used for unhooking and weighing big pike, the catfish was tipped softly and easily head first into the water - although how he might eventually be taken out was a problem that had not yet been addressed. He showed no immediate demur for having his surroundings further restricted than even the little pond that had become his temporary residence, although it would be hard to truly imagine what he was thinking of the whole business - especially when a specialist vet from Defra jabbed him with a sharp instrument to take tissue samples away to test in case he was carrying pathogens that might stop him being exported.

Tipton, who was masterminding the netting and transfer with Kendal, had disappeared once it was clear that everything was going smoothly. Suddenly he appeared again, carrying a swishing bucket.

"What's that?" Kendal asked, curious, as Tipton put it up on the lorry bed and clambered up the stepladder to join it - not so easy for a man of his age. He then proceeded to heave the bucket up and tip the contents into Gobblemouth's tank.

"Oh, just a little treat for him - some Brightwell spring water from our new borehole. Might bring us a bit of luck too - I doubt if everything will be rosy along the way."

Kendal dropped Gobblemouth a fresh herring and was glad to see it vanish: a good appetite meant a healthy fish. They readied the truck for stocking the other containers first thing in the morning and left Gobblemouth on his own as darkness fell.

***

Some little time later the big fish felt a vibration through the truck bed: somebody had climbed up beside his tank. A dark shape loomed over the translucent lid, and it was raised stealthily. An arm holding a package reached in and pushed it against the side of the tank where it stuck fast, well out of sight of anyone who might look in from above. The arm was quickly withdrawn and Gobblemouth heard somebody drop lightly down from the truck and creep away.

***

Departure day was a little bit of an anti-climax, and it was wet and windy which did not seem at all auspicious. "Well, never mind the weather," said a dripping Tipton before they all got into their vehicles to set of in convoy. The title of one of his favourite books came to his lips: "Fair stood the wind for France."

Unbidden, a memory of setting the throttle and trim of his Stirling for a bombing raid deep into the Continent almost brought a tear to his eye, not least for the good friends who had perished in the desperate missions. The octogenarian earl cleared a lump from his throat and added: "Good luck everyone."

Helen, Giles' son Mark, Roger Percy, Mike's mother Carol Cook and Bryn Thomas waved them all off at the estate gates. Soon the convoy was speeding for the south coast.

It would have been hard not to feel elated once they were under way, although as travelling companions the group still had lots to learn about one another. Everyone looked happy, except perhaps for Pedro DeAvila, who as usual was completely unreadable.

Chapter 6

Mark Kendal was not the only one to have suspicions about Pedro DeAvila: Derek Jones was also wary. Derek had been transport driver for Percy enterprises for 12 years, and during that time he had worked with four co-drivers, getting along with all of them. His usual regular driver's mate-cum-navigator was Peter Wonnacot, an ex-smokery employee who had shared quite a few overseas trips with him. He had grown to rely on him, but unfortunately for this particular project Peter was on maternity leave to help his wife with their newborn first child, a daughter. Derek found DeAvila an adequate temporary substitute work-wise, but no more than that - despite a veneer of friendliness the man was a closed book, not at all forthcoming about himself in any way. And he spent an awful lot of time talking on his mobile phone, sometimes pointedly walking out of earshot and often speaking in at least a couple of languages Derek did not know as well as one he recognised as Spanish.

Before the big adventure that was now underway, Derek and DeAvila had fitted in three UK round trips together by way of training, and he had nothing to complain about so far as the man's driving skills were concerned, nor about his willingness to do a good workmanlike job - he threw himself into any tasks with energy and without complaint. And on their coming overseas trip together, of course, his language skills might well prove very useful.

All the same there had been incidents that raised Derek's worries. For example, in a service station cafe near Liverpool on a recent delivery trip, DeAvila had talked to a group of shifty-looking men and then disappeared with them for a short while.

"Old friends," was all he said by way of explanation on his return. To Derek, it had looked more like a planned rendezvous.

And then there was the toolbox incident. Under the truck bed and fastened to the chassis just ahead of the big fuel tank, the big metal container held essentials like jacks, tyre levers and wrenches for wheel nuts and the hydraulic connectors. It was kept firmly locked so that none of this vital equipment went astray. In spite of this Derek checked the contents regularly 'just to be on the safe side'. One day, however, he had found it unlocked when he was sure he had secured it. Since the toolbox key was on the same keyring as the tractor's ignition key and since both men shared this, he asked DeAvila if he had opened the box.

The man shook his head.

"No. I never looked inside, not ever."

As usual, his quick eyes darted everywhere except directly at his inquisitor.

***

The trip down to Poole for the Brittany Ferries crossing to Cherbourg was uneventful and fast in spite of the rain, and once aboard they all gathered for a meal in the self-service lounge, the notable exception being DeAvila who had sloped off after arriving.

"Here's to us!"

Tipton raised his glass and they toasted the enterprise.

***

Mike Cook spent a restless night. He had opted to sleep in a sleeping-lounge reclining chair rather than a cabin, and when he woke again for what seemed like the millionth time and heard the rest of the ship's compliment waking up, he took himself to the washroom before it got too busy, washed and dressed for the day ahead, and then went out to find the highest deck to watch their approach to the port. At the top of the companionway he stopped dead: leaning on the rail was Vicky Price.

While he was quite able to break the ice with almost anybody when he was at work, there were times when he found talking with young women of around his own age excruciatingly awkward. He'd met Vicky during the trip preparations, of course, and had even shaken hands with her. But those lovely frank light blue eyes were so engaging he had to look away whenever their glances met, mainly for fear that she might think he was staring. Which was what his instincts told him to do - stare. It was all so difficult. Should he go up to her directly and say hello? Should he perhaps go to the rail somewhere near her so that she might look around and see him? Should he go to the other side of the ship and pretend he had not seen her at all?

All these thoughts became academic when she turned suddenly, saw him and smiled. He felt himself colouring.

"Come over and see," she said. "Look, we're nearly there."

It was, they agreed afterwards, one of the most exciting moments they had ever had, standing side by side watching the big ship gently edging into the dock and knowing they would soon be trundling off into France and beyond, much much further than either of them had ever travelled by road in one go. Mike wanted the moment to last and last, but all too soon the loudspeakers started calling for passengers to prepare to disembark. Going ahead of her down the companionway he felt a tap on his shoulder. He turned to find her grinning down at him.

"I don't bite you know."

In that moment he knew they were going to be good friends. And perhaps ... well, who knows?

***

Whatever Pedro DeAvila had been up to during the crossing, he was back, present and correct, as they climbed again into the vehicles.

Vicky rode in the truck cab along with Derek Jones when they left the ferry and headed for customs clearance, while DeAvila took her place in Tipton's Range Rover. They hoped to be waved through but the French authorities pored over the paperwork and asked Vicky question after question, even though Roger Percy had done his level best to make sure the path ahead of them was well cleared. The fish tanks also had to be inspected, the officials decided. This inspection apparently included a head-count of everything in the containers: difficult enough with even the larger fish, but when he saw the customs team attempting to count a tank full of darting small fish, Derek had to turn aside and suppress a snigger. Not surprisingly, this task was quickly abandoned. When one of the team opened Gobblemouth's container and peered in, he gave a low whistle. It brought the others to his side and they talked excitedly for some minutes before retreating - only for one of them to pick up a telephone and spend yet more minutes in an animated conversation. When he put it down he told Derek and Vicky they would have to wait a little longer.

"Wouldn't you know it - had to be us they picked on," said Derek as other trucks left the vessel and sped off into France. "It's that monster's fault. This is the last time I agree to be chauffeur to a giant catfish."

It was a good fifteen minutes, in fact, before a little dark blue Peugeot came beetling across the now rapidly-emptying port forecourt and disgorged yet another official who was led immediately to the tanker and to Gobblemouth. Like his companions before, however, he failed to notice the tank's well-obscured clandestinely-delivered package. Then the small and rather tubby official approached the pair waiting in the tanker cab. He had bushy black eyebrows but the slicked down black hair on his head made Vicky think immediately it was a wig. He also had a thin black moustache which twitched when he spoke. She tried not to laugh at the comic effect.

59

"You may go now," he said slowly, but with only slightly accented English diction. "But under no circumstances must the big fish be let loose in any French water, by accident or design. Any French water - do you understand? This is most important. To do so would be very serious. Any problems which make this a possibility must be reported immediately to me. Here..."

He reached in his pocket and pulled out a card, passed it to Vicky.

"Call the number at the bottom here. As you can see, my name is Claude Moreau, inspector. That is all, please. I am sorry for the delay."

They assured him they would call and he touched his forehead, and then at last they were on their way.

***

"I thought our civil servants were bad enough," said Tipton, tut-tutting as he waited for the truck in the parking area.

The port had virtually emptied before the fish transporter at last came trundling towards them. Tipton and Giles exchanged an untalkative DeAvila for Vicky before setting off.

"Now Giles," cautioned Tipton unnecessarily, "remember what side of the road you're supposed to be driving on."

"Mais oui, mon frere," said Giles. "D'accord."

A few miles out of town with the Range Rover riding shotgun to the transporter, Giles turned to Tipton and said: "I say, bro, don't look now, but I think we're being followed."

A minute later, Vicky sneaked a look back, as did Tipton. Keeping a discreet distance behind them but nevertheless following their every twist and turn was a little dark blue Peugeot.

***

Tipton insisted on a good meal and rest break in the first day's journey even though they had lost time over the paperwork at the port. Vicky and Mike were particularly glad of this because they had both missed breakfast on the boat. After that, the rest of the afternoon drive to a spot south of Vierzon was smooth and the weather improved considerably. They all parked up in brilliant late sunshine and gathered in the hotel for supper. As there were other dark blue Peugeots in the area it would have been hard to tell if one of them had been following, and Vicky saw no sign of the little official who had cautioned them at the port.

Before they ate Vicky asked Mike if he could join her at a bar table - she had lugged her bulging briefcase and laptop along and immediately fired up the machine.

"I'm a bit worried," she said, frowning prettily and taking out some papers. "I'm the only one who knows about all this, so what would happen if anything happened to me? Strikes me, that would be the end of it. Would you mind if I gave you a bit of a briefing on what to do with it all just in case? In know it's probably the last thing you want to do right now, but it would be a big weight off my mind, really."

Mike had been about to compose a blog to send back to his paper, but how could he refuse?

Watching them, Tipton leaned across his table to Mark Kendal.

"Bit of a romance starting up there, d'you think?" he said, nodding towards the pair with their heads together studying a pile of forms.

Kendal smiled.

"I wouldn't be a bit surprised."

***

At the lorry park, Kendal and Derek Jones inspected the fish the next morning while the others were finishing their breakfast. All appeared well. The trout looked lively enough, as did the baby char, and all the monitors were spot-on.

"No casualties," observed Derek Jones. "I hate casualties, but sometimes it's inevitable, especially if we get delayed. I was a bit worried too about the extra motion aboard the ferry, but it doesn't seem to have done them any harm. When we do get dead fish it isn't always possible at the time to tell what caused it, so I usually take them back to our depot for a post-mortem."

Gobblemouth too appeared to be unruffled by the journey so far, though what he made of solitary confinement in his custom-made home nobody would be able to tell. Kendal fed him a herring which quickly disappeared, as if it had been vacuumed up. The big fish then sank to the bottom of the tank and lay inert, digesting. Had he been able to talk - and indeed if he had a long enough memory for such things - he might have told the pair that he had made a journey across the Channel and indeed France once before, long ago and in the other direction.

***

"Not that we get many casualties," Jones added.

Coming down from the tanker, Kendal asked: "Is it a difficult rig to drive? I mean, you've got all that water slopping around. Doesn't that make a difference to the way it handles?"

Jones flashed a smile, rare for him. "Only if you're new to it," he said, patting one of the giant opaque plastic tanks arranged in pairs along the truck bed. "The main difference is all this liquid wants to go in a straight line once it's on the move, especially when you get some speed up. And it's not too happy with stopping when you put the brakes on, either. Like most things, you get used to it. Experience of driving rigs like petrol tankers helps. DeAvila has been a tanker driver, so he was able to adapt quite easy, like. I suppose in a way we're lucky to have him."

He looked towards the hotel, across the main road from the lorry park.

62

"Talking of DeAvila, I wonder where he is now? We're about due to start."

As he spoke, the man in question appeared crossing the tarmac from the direction of the road, talking animatedly on his phone. Closer, as he put the phone away and acknowledged them, Kendal set off back across the road to pick up Mike and get his van rolling. The sun was already quite high and it was getting warm. He felt it was going to be a good day.

Chapter 7

But now this, a campsite accident. Tipton was barely conscious when the paramedics rolled him into a stretcher to lift him into the emergency unit, but they worked swiftly and identified a badly broken lower left leg and slight concussion. He was coming round swiftly, however, while they strapped up the double fracture and immobilised his leg. He would need further treatment that could either be arranged at Perigueux or at home in England, but they insisted there would be no way he could carry on his journey, especially at his age - "*Absolutement non!*"

Even the painkillers couldn't cushion his disappointment.

"There's nothing worse than feeling old and useless," he said wryly to Giles while they were waiting for instructions from the travel insurance people.

"You've been through worse and you're a tough old bugger. At least you're alive."

Giles's phone rang. A plane to take him home was being arranged. As they were somewhere between airports at Perigueux and Toulouse, which would they prefer?

Giles picked the latter.

"Can somebody fly with him, please? We'd prefer that," was the next request to worry over.

A simple "Yes" solved the immediate problem, but a council of war was clearly necessary to decide not only who the "somebody" should be but how they were going to carry on with the loss of two members of the team. Under the circumstances, the continuation of the trip beyond delivery of the trout and char now looked like a folly too far. Was this to be the end of the Quest for the Crimson Trout, and indeed the overdue return of one of the Danube's residents that went along with it?

It was nearly dawn when they got Tipton back to his hotel and gathered around his bed.

"Oh, hello. Which of you is going to read the last rights?" the waking invalid said.

Giles put his cards on the table.

"Look, my brother and I are the least useful parts of this operation as far as I see it. If you, Kendal, can find extra space to give Vicky a lift for the time being, I can whip him off to Toulouse first thing and go with him on the plane to England. Simple. I can come back for the car any time I like once he's safely in hospital."

"I could. But it's dodgy, not to say illegal. Vicky would be in the back without a safety belt. And aren't you forgetting the lorry has two drivers, by the way? Perhaps Derek or Pedro could drive you and your brother to the airport while we get on our way. They could drive on to rendezvous with us and we'd still have the benefit of the Range Rover as a back-up vehicle."

Giles thought it over. "I see your point," he said.

"Can I say something?" The small voice came from Vicky, who until then had been holding Tipton's hand and taking on the role of nurse.

"If one of you could get me and Mr Tipton to the airport, I could go with him to England. I've had some nursing training that might be helpful and I think that's the most useful thing I can do. That would free you, Giles. I've shown Mike Cook what to do with all the paperwork and I'm sure he could cope with that."

They all looked at her in silence.

"Well, what about it?"

65

The implications of this suggestion struck Mike particularly hard. Vicky's offer was practical and good, but it would mean her part in the adventure was over, which was hardly fair - plus he'd be losing a lively and engaging companion, and just a brief time after meeting her at that. All the same, he had to admit that the circumstances they faced now that Tipton had been injured were exceptional, and that called for exceptional measures. He realised also that he had no real say in the matter.

"Would you? It would be an enormous sacrifice, giving up the trip," said Giles. "I'm sure my brother would be delighted to have you with him, but he could just as well put up with me, ugly though I am."

Tipton smiled from his bed and Vicky looked round the faces. "Of course it'll be a disappointment," she said frankly. "But I wouldn't like to go on knowing I hadn't stepped up to the mark when needed, really I wouldn't."

That settled it. The fish truck and the campervan were moved up to the hotel and they all agreed to try to take a nap before putting the plan into action. But Mike found he could not switch off and went into the hotel garden where he found Vicky sitting with her elbows on a cafe table looking at the rising sun, which was already beginning to warm the air.

"Beautiful, isn't it?" she said as he joined her and sat. "It is a wrench to turn my back on all this, but it is the most sensible thing to do."

She put a hand on his arm and squeezed gently.

"I'm sure there will be other times, other adventures."

For that moment, she seemed far older than her years. To deny that this was absolutely the right thing to do would turn him into a wheedling infant. Without warning she leaned closer and kissed his cheek gently, the barest brush of soft lips. "Good luck," she said. "I know you'll all do fine."

She rose and went, leaving him staring at a bed of sunlit geraniums which momentarily merged into a swimming sea of watery red.

***

Before they left, the chief of police arrived and told Derek to be careful for the rest of his journey through France - thefts from vehicles, particularly those with foreign plates, were on the increase: the truck and its cargo should be guarded at all times. He also reported on their investigations so far.

"A travelling fair, the police said," Derek told Kendal. "Nasty little fish-snaffling buggers. They were moved on. The Gendarmes wanted us to stay and lay charges but we explained we could lose all our fish if they stayed in the tanks too long, so they let everyone go with a caution. They must have been tired - normally it isn't so easy to get away and once French officialdom kicks in you could be trapped for months. Lucky for the travellers too. Gipsies, really. I bet they couldn't believe their luck when they found a fish supper served up for them."

While the engine warmed up Kendal asked if the truck was damaged: there had been some minor tinkering with the dashboard wiring that was easy enough to fix, Derek said, so the only real loss was a few trout. He was about to climb into the cab when they noticed DeAvila was again missing.

Animated voices made them look across the hotel car park towards a car towing a caravan that had just pulled in. Pedro DeAvila was talking with a dark-haired woman who had stepped down out of the car. As they watched, the pair walked further away from earshot, their conversation punctuated with much gesturing on the woman's part. Then they turned, DeAvila acknowledging the fact that people were waiting for him with a wave. The woman clutched briefly at his arm before going back to her vehicle.

"A friend of yours?" Jones asked, and characteristically DeAvila's eyes turned away.

"Just saying hello. Are we ready to go?"

***

Two miles down the road there was an incident which did not seem very odd at the time - a small white van steered ahead of them just before a roundabout. There was no traffic on the roundabout to make it stop but it did - and there it stalled. While a grinding of the starter motor told them the driver was trying his best to restart, traffic began to build up behind. To a chorus of impatient toots the driver and a companion then climbed out of the disabled vehicle, lifted its bonnet and started poking around inside. The people now parked behind the fish transporter also started getting out and walking forward to see what was going on, and quite a crowd was soon milling around the truck, some even leaning on it. After a few more minutes the van crew suddenly emerged from their study of the engine compartment and climbed back in their stalled vehicle. It started briskly and they drove it away, onto the roundabout, carrying on to the left and away from the exit the transporter took. Oddly, once the transporter itself entered the roundabout, Derek noticed in his mirror that the van had gone right around it and was now half a dozen vehicles behind.

***

The surprise of seeing the snow-topped Pyrenees for the first time almost made Mike Cook forget that Vicky Price was now absent from the party. They had been driving steadily south for some time and he had been asleep for some of the trip. When Kendal said: "Look at that Mike - beautiful, eh?" he lifted his eyes, and where there had once been an empty skyline the imposing range reared up to incredible heights.

"Wow," was all he could say, and Kendal laughed. It was one sight among many that had already impressed the young man on his first visit, with France putting on a brilliant autumnal show: avenues of poplar, plane and chestnut trees changing colour against a clear blue sky, pickers at work in the rolling vineyards overlooked by fairytale

68

chateaux, and huge harvesters trailing clouds of dust over golden-ripe cereal crops. But the sight of the white peaks topped all that.

"I felt that the first time I saw them too," Kendal said.

They were on a fast highway and well ahead of the transporter. The Range Rover had passed them some time ago with a toot and a wave from Giles, who after seeing Tipton and Vicky on the plane was now speeding to the rendezvous to make sure everything was ready for the fish handover.

"We're coming into the Arriege," Kendal explained. "We can stop for a coffee and a snack just outside Mirepoix - take a look at the map - where there's a pizza and fried chicken cafe. When we're over these hills there's just one more valley before the mountains, but we won't be going over those. The exchange is at Foix, one of the bigger towns, and from then on we head east for the unknown part of the whole trip. I'm quite excited about that - are you?"

Mike sensed Kendal was trying to help him look forward, forget about Vicky for a while. Forget for the moment about Tipton too - they'd all miss the likeable earl who had a real knack for keeping everyone's spirits up.

"I guess you're OK with the paperwork?" Kendal said, reminding him of his new responsibilities.

Mike shrugged. "As ready as I'll ever be. There's a lot to do but it's all mostly straightforward. Vicky said every one piece of paper in this bag represents another ten she had to process before we started out. I'll have another look at them when we stop."

Deep down he was shy, in spite of his apparent ease with people he talked to in his job. He was still not yet comfortable calling Kendal 'Mark' even though the man insisted he should drop the formal 'Mr Kendal' he had been using since they started. Mike got round this little awkwardness by adapting his conversation to exclude both the formal address and Kendal's first name.

He tried looking at the papers but found reading anything while he was in motion gave him a queezy stomach. Even looking briefly at the map had started to produce butterflies so he put it all aside and concentrated on looking ahead at the growing hills. From the highway they shifted onto smaller and slower rural roads bordered with wayside wildflowers.

Twenty minutes after arriving at their pit-stop cafe, the transporter drew up and they greeted Derek Jones and Pedro DeAvila, who parked behind the building and went on inside for a quick bite and a drink. They made their own tea on the campervan stove and waited outside in the sunshine. Kendal looked very tired, Mike thought - indeed, none of them had really slept at all. Even after they had delivered the fish, an exercise that would take up most of the afternoon, there was still some way to go before they got to their pre-booked accommodation. At least they would sleep well on the coming night!

Through half-closed eyes Mike watched a dark-haired woman in a red blouse and jeans come around a corner of the cafe building. She looked around for a moment, cautiously, he thought, then turned and disappeared. At that moment Jones and DeAvila emerged from the cafe and Mike reached out to shake Kendal's shoulder gently to wake him. It was time to hit the road again and now that they were heading into the mountains they kept well behind the transporter so that they could quickly catch up and help if it ran into any problems.

***

Not far away, seated in a dark blue Peugeot, another figure watched the whole episode.

***

A jazz festival was in full swing when they arrived in Foix and Mike had vivid first impressions of packed streets around a prominent castle on a mound above the town, and music from a stage set to the side of central gardens. Through it all threaded a mountain stream that was flexing its muscles and about to swell into a broad river. Bent on business, they felt like intruders in the gay scene, especially when they had to negotiate the heavy traffic and thronging pedestrians with the big fish transporter. It was with some relief that they eased their way out of this melee and took the rising country road to the fish farm where the exchange was to take place.

On the way, Mike was surprised to see the transporter parked at a wayside cafe on the outskirts of a tiny hamlet. They very nearly sped past it without noticing, and had to reverse some way in order to pull off the road beside it. DeAvila was about to climb in the driver's seat; Derek Jones appeared to be snoozing, which was not all that surprising.

"Just checking," said DeAvila. "I thought we might have lost some tyre pressure in the back left set but everything looks OK. I'll see you at the farm."

And with that he was off. But as the campervan was about to pull away and follow, a figure hovering in the cafe doorway caught Mike's eye. A woman, dark, in a red blouse, seemed to be watching them. His mind put two images together: she looked very much like the woman he had seen at the other cafe earlier that afternoon. For it to be the same woman would be quite a coincidence, but although he tried to put both images out of his head as inconsequential, they kept popping up again to nag him. After a while he said to Mark Kendal: "Is this the road we have to come back along or do we drive on from the other side of the farm?"

"I think it's the only road," said Kendal. "If we drove on we'd be in Spain, no time at all. Why?"

"No matter."

***

The actual transfer took place smoothly and quickly, a 'must' for fish handling, but there was enough to do to keep everyone busy. Mike and Giles took the paperwork to the farm manager in a little

71

wooden hut that served as an office while DeAvila and Derek Jones helped two of the farm workers manage the fish, an operation which took a lot of gesturing because of the language barriers. While DeAvila's French hadn't seemed all that bad on the way down, he clearly had some difficulties with the local dialect. He was also not as patient as his colleague, and some of the language he used didn't need interpretation.

Thoughtfully the fish farm manager had laid on a tray of sandwiches and beers for everyone once they stepped out of the stuffy little hut that reeked of creosote, and they sat around to eat on crates and tubs in the early evening sunshine before, once again, it was time to head off: now they would be travelling due East, quickly as possible, stopping near Carcassonne for a very well earned rest. Once again, Mike and Kendal would ride shotgun. Although Giles had offered him a ride in the Range Rover for a change, Mike sensed that Kendal was glad of the companionship he had provided, so for the time being decided the arrangement was fine. Giles again sped off to pave the way ahead and while DeAvila and Derek Jones checked the lorry over and headed off Mike used the fish farm's wifi system to send a quick message to Tipton via Vicky's laptop: all was well, he reported, and phase two of the adventure had started. He knew it was news Tipton would like to hear, even if he might curse the fact that he was no longer a part of it.

"Please give my best wishes to Vicky," he concluded, and then, after a moment's thought, "and tell her I wish she was here."

That duty completed, he quickly filed another brief log to his paper.

***

Oddly, they found the transporter had pulled in once again at the same wayside cafe it stopped at earlier in the day. DeAvila was just climbing into the cab, so they simply hovered to wait for it to move ahead again. Of the woman Mike had seen earlier in the day there was no sign, but this time the transporter's second impromptu stop at the very same spot reawakened Mike's earlier suspicions. He was sure there was something going on, and that 'something' had a lot to do with DeAvila - but could not put his finger on what it might be. Should he alert any of the others, he wondered? Not until he had a clearer idea of what it might be, he told himself - above all, he did not want to look a fool.

The mechanical voice from Kendal's Satnav cut though his thoughts: "*In 300 yards, cross the roundabout, second exit.*"

Mike checked out the roundabout signs. Ahead, through a series of neat and quaintly ancient hamlets, lay the walled and turreted town of Carcassonne, and beyond that more and more unfamiliar sights - and other countries.

Chapter 8

Back in England, Tipton was more annoyed with himself than he was with his broken leg. It was mending, however, and he had some mobility with the aid of a crutch.

He really hadn't enjoyed the brief spell in hospital while they got the bone aligned and plastered him up, for it reminded him too much of times past - not the enjoyable moments either.

"At the back of your mind there's always the feeling things aren't going to get any better," he confided to Helen. Wisely, her only comment was: "Well, more often than not they do get better, don't they?"

Bryn Thomas, in the meantime, had been busy looking into the gold figurine that had been found along with Gobblemouth in his muddy lair. Because of its possible value he'd had to inform the coroner, he reported to Tipton, and there was the likelihood of a Treasure Trove inquest to decide its fate.

"Well, actually, that's not quite true," he said. "I mean, the 'Treasure Trove' law as everyone probably knows it no longer exists in England. It was replaced in 1996 by the Treasure Act, and the main difference from Treasure Trove is the removal of a stipulation that finders had to prove whether or not finds had been hidden on purpose so that they could be recovered later. It still requires a sort-of inquest though."

Tipton raised his eyebrows. "Mighty difficult to prove anything like that, even with your theory of votive offerings."

"Mmm," agreed Bryn Thomas. "That's undoubtedly what it is, and I would dearly like to know the story behind it. I may be second-guessing the coroner but the good news is you can probably keep it, or if you like donate it to the British Museum - they'd pay you what they think it is worth - or even the county archive. I take it you don't want to just sell it?"

"Money's always useful, but no, I don't think we're that hard up. Not yet anyway. No, it can go on display with Nudd's hound. Are the two are related?"

Nudd's Hound was a beautiful translucent green stone carving of a hunting dog, and like the kneeling golden girl it had been found on the estate a few years back, possibly going a long way towards saving Brightwell's lovely grounds from compulsory purchase and development as a housing estate. The hound's finder had been none other than Mike Cook, currently ploughing across France helping to deliver Gobblemouth to his home waters.

The Welshman frowned. "Well, no - not definitely, anyway. I'm working on it. Whatever reason it was found here is another piece of the complex story of Brightwell's past. When I'm a little bit surer of everything I'll tell you all I know."

"I look forward to that," said Tipton. However, for the moment, he could not stop his thoughts quickly straying back to France, but this was short-lived because the telephone started to ring. As usual he left it in case it was one of Helen's friends calling her, or perhaps a booking for the retreat which one of the staff could deal with, but she quickly shouted up for him to take the call.

"Who is it?"

"I don't know. But he said he was from the Foreign Office. Wants to know if he could come and see you."

Tipton frowned - it was a long time since he'd had anything to do with the sort of business the Foreign Office handled. Anxiety swiftly followed - had anything happened to the fish truck or the people travelling with it??

"Hello - is anything wrong?" he said before the caller had even introduced himself in a cultured Civil Service voice.

"No - no, nothing at all sir," the caller said. "I expect you're thinking of your friends in France are you? Well, it's certainly what I'm calling about, but there is no trouble whatsoever so please put your mind at rest. However I do need to come down and discuss something with you - would tomorrow morning be all right? I can be there by about 11. Name's Simon Jenkins, by the way."

"What's it about?"

But the man would not say, at least not on the phone.

"I'll keep that until tomorrow - I hope you don't mind," he said.

Once he had put the phone down Tipton's immediate relief that there was nothing wrong with the French trip was quickly replaced with a new worry about what exactly he or they might have done to attract the attention of the Foreign Office. It was a worry he would have to carry until the following morning.

***

The crimson trout questers had a rambling holiday cottage for their next stopover. Owned by family friends of the Tiptons, it slept eight people in various rooms - even more if the two lounge sofa-beds were used - and had a large salt-water swimming pool which most of the hot and by now very tired travellers were glad to take advantage of. Some of them anyway - DeAvila abstained and so did Mark Kendal, who said: "I've a horror of being totally immersed in water." Since hearing the story of his Scottish big-pike catch during which he very nearly drowned, the others could well understand his reluctance.

Earlier, they'd done a big shop for supplies at a Super-U, and while the others were having a good splash, Kendal and DeAvila cooked up an excellent chicken, peppers and tinned tomato stew with a big pot of rice, bread and a dish of fresh salad to accompany it. There was cheese and fruit to follow. Eaten on the terrace, it was all washed down with a copious quantity of local red wine amid high spirits. The two cooks got on surprisingly well together, but everyone was slightly surprised when, halfway through the meal, Kendal raised his glass and said: "Here's to Pedro, the best Spanish chef in the South of France."

It was the first time most of them had seen DeAvila smile, and he did so with an uncharacteristic blush that darkened his already swarthy complexion. Mike Cook was probably not alone in wondering if he should revise his opinion of the truck co-driver, but when the man excused himself towards the end of the meal and still had not reappeared by the time they were loading up the dishwasher, Mike felt the moment might be right to share his suspicions about the Spaniard with Kendal. Seizing a chance when they were outside alone on the terrace together, Mike asked Kendal what he really thought about the truck co-driver.

"Well, actually, I think he has hidden depths. He's a bit secretive about himself, I suppose, but I'm sure he has good reasons for that. At first it worried me but I'm coming to the conclusion he's playing a part rather than being the man I think he is. And he could be a bit shy. Why do you ask?"

"I'm afraid I've been thinking he's up to no good."

"Oh?" Kendal looked at him searchingly. "Really? Why?"

"I think there's a stowaway on the lorry and I think he knows all about it. A woman."

Kendal tipped his head to one side and Mike told him about the sightings at the cafe stops - incidents Kendal clearly hadn't noticed himself, at least not consciously.

"I'm sure it's the same clothes, the same woman," he concluded. "And I think that's where he is now."

"Whoa!" said Kendal, "You can't go around making wild accusations against people, you know. But saying you're right...what do we do? Perhaps we ought to go and see what he's up to now - at least that will clear things up for both of us. What do you think?"

"I think we should too. I know it feels a bit sneaky, but we can easily hide ourselves from the lorry if we circle round and duck through the next-door vineyard. It's nearly dark now and that'll help."

And indeed feeling conspiratorial and more than a little underhand, they slipped quietly off the terrace and into the adjacent field.

The vineyard was alive with rustlings and the chirrups of cicadas, which had decided to stay up and give a late concert. There was also the unpleasant sensation of walking through trailing spider silk, and a personal cloud of midges attended each of them to make them wish they hadn't embarked on the foray. However, once they were near the lorry they could hear voices, which made them forget the minor discomforts.

Once they were closer, they parted big vine leaves to peer through a barbed-wire fence into the orchard where the lorry was parked. DeAvila was clearly visible, sitting on the edge of the trailer bed between the tank stays, swinging his legs. And in the opened doorway of the tackle cabin stood a woman, as Mike had predicted. The pair were talking softly together.

"Who is she?" Kendal whispered.

"I think she was at the campsite when the lorry was stolen," said Mike. "She was talking with DeAvila there. And I saw her again when the truck stopped at a cafe the next day, and then again at another cafe. I think she's been hiding in the cabin all this time and sneaking on and off to feed herself ... with DeAvila's help of course."

Kendal was about to ask Mike what they ought to do next when a vehicle's lights flickered across the scene, making them both duck. The beam came from a vehicle on the approach road to the property, but as it neared the dwelling the lights went out and the car continued on, moving slowly and quietly. Kendal and Mike held their breaths as a small dark-coloured Peugeot nosed towards the lorry and stopped not far away.

"Hello - now what's going on?" Kendal whispered. The pair watched intently, hardly daring to breathe. Astonishingly, DeAvila and the woman, who must also have seen the vehicle approaching, had not moved at all!

"Well, I'm blowed," Kendal uttered softly, as to their amazement the car door opened and a short, stocky figure got out to approach DeAvila, who pushed himself off the truck bed to jump to the ground. The two went up to each other, shook hands and clapped one another on the back, and motioned the woman to join them. DeAvila held her hand to steady her jump down and the newcomer formally embraced her.

"They all know each other!" said Mike, astonished.

"Yes. He's the man that French customs sent for when we arrived in port in France. Claude Moreau, I think that's his name. And I'm pretty sure he's been following us all this time."

The strange meeting lasted no more than a few minutes after which the men shook hands again before the newcomer climbed back in his car and quietly drove back to the road, lights still extinguished. As he did so DeAvila helped the stowaway back up on to the lorry where she entered the tackle cabin and shut the door behind her. Then DeAvila turned and started back towards the cottage.

"What now?" asked Kendal, still whispering.

"I don't know. But let's get back now - don't want to arouse his suspicions, do we? We'll have to find out what the others think."

Before they entered they agreed that it would be best if they could tell both companions their news at the same time, with DeAvila out of earshot of course. The man in question was sitting at the kitchen table finishing some of the leftovers while Derek Jones and Giles put away clean crockery.

"That ruddy man's got the appetite of a camel," said Jones in an aside to Mike and Kendal. "When he went out to check the truck he had a damn great cheese sandwich with him."

But with him sitting there, it wasn't the moment to break into the story. Neither did an opportunity come soon. Whenever the time seemed right DeAvila would pop up, irritatingly just within earshot.

But the chance did come the next morning when it was decided to fuel up the truck so that they could have an unbroken couple of days driving without lengthy stops. Jones and DeAvila were about to set off for a nearby Texaco station together when Kendal seized the moment and suggested DeAvila could do this alone. "I'd like you to come and take a look at the brook on the other side of the vineyard," he said to Derek. "There's some enormous fish in it. Maybe you can help me find out what they are."

In the end all four of them went on the brook expedition, and when Kendal heard the engine noise dwindle in the distance, he and Mike told the others all about the stowaway and the odd night-time meeting. Giles and Jones were astonished - they clearly hadn't suspected anything themselves.

"You're sure?" was Giles' reaction.

Jones was incredulous. "What? Just behind me in the cabin while I was driving? I don't believe it - you're not pulling my wotsit, are you? And what's that Frenchman up to? What's going on? What are we going to do?"

***

Nearly 900 miles away in the green heart of England, Tipton was being told: "We think it's time we informed you and your crew. We can replace your folk with our own agents of course, but if they choose otherwise it's important they behave absolutely as normal, as if they don't suspect a thing. The critical period will be crossing into Italy, where we're sure there are Mafia links, but there could be approaches anytime from now on until they cross the border with Slovenia on the other side."

This dark turn of events took Tipton by surprise and it was a lot to digest all at once. His first surprise had been that Simon Jenkins, the man from the Ministry, had arrived with a sheepish-looking Roger Percy, the owner of the fish truck. Vicky Price was with them too, but as Tipton was about to find out, she too had been in the dark about what was going on until this moment. More shocks for Tipton followed: Roger had been in on the subterfuge from around the time DeAvila was recruited, and the object of the exercise was to draw out people involved in a lucrative people-smuggling chain that led all the way to Slovenia and Croatia and perhaps far beyond.

"I'm sorry, sir, you've a right to be upset," said Jenkins. "The only unforeseen thing that came up was you breaking your leg, for which we can't be blamed. But there was no way we could make everything look authentic if everyone knew what was going on. We're dealing with a sophisticated outfit, with money going in and out of the UK - freshly laundered here of course - and people also being transported back and forth. Illegal immigrants pay a lot to come and live in England, and there are people who want to get out and get 'lost' for various reasons, chiefly running from justice. The French authorities are involved and they've had agents following your consignment all along. And in case you're worried by the danger aspect, we also have an agent on the case."

"You do?" Another shock.

"We do. You know him as Pedro DeAvila."

***

At that moment, the man known as Pedro DeAvila had just re-entered the cottage to find himself surrounded by untrusting glowers. However, to the great surprise of his accusers his face broke into a huge grin as soon as he was aware his cover had been blown. Even more surprisingly, his voice had dropped its accent and the man now spoke in perfect English.

"Of course, you're correct - and of course you should have an explanation," he said. "In fact, around about now the whole situation is being explained to Michael Tipton back in England. But the first thing you should know is that you have been very useful in an operation to flush out an international smuggling conspiracy..."

A knock at the door interrupted him, and he nodded to Mike.

"Can you let him in? I think that's the French connection - friendly of course. There should be somebody else with him too. It's time you all met her."

Surprised into silence by the transformation of Pedro DeAvila - the man had even dropped his furtive behaviour - Mike, Kendal, Derek Jones and Giles looked as if they had been frozen. Mike went to the door with a deep sense of bewilderment, but he did not feel greatly shocked to see the stout little moustachioed Frenchman. However he was quite stricken by the beauty of the woman who stood behind him - a woman he had only seen fleetingly before, and in half-light. Dark-skinned, she had flashing black eyes and a wide smile that went with it, an effect that was immediately engaging.

"Bonjour. Entrez, s'il vous plait," he said in his best French when he managed to find his tongue.

"Thank you," the Frenchman replied in English, while the woman gave him a broad wink.

"Can we all sit down and relax a bit, do you think?" said DeAvila when Mike led the newcomers in.

"I'll put some more coffee on," said Giles, sensing the episode was going to take some time. He busied himself in the adjacent open plan kitchen while Moreau said good morning to everyone and introduced Zofia Balorengre, who gave a little curtsey before sitting down.

"I'm afraid it was really necessary to be secretive to this point, even though it was arranged some time back before you left England," said DeAvila. "Roger Percy was really helpful when we first went to him, and it's thanks to him really that we've got this far."

"You mean my boss knew about it all along? The bastard!" said Derek Jones, now even more incredulous.

"I'm afraid so. But the fact is the contacts these smugglers have made with me so far have really helped efforts to map the extent of their operation ... and it's beginning to look very big indeed. So much so, in fact, that it could begin to get dangerous as we approach the important borders you are set to cross, first into Italy tomorrow and then Slovenia and across Croatia to the border by the Danube. Our bosses in England and France have decided to ask all of you if you would like to be replaced by our own agents from tomorrow on. In fact some are being briefed right now. We'll arrange a passage back to England for you, and expenses on the way. What do you think?"

In the awkward silence that followed Giles brought over cups, hot milk and two jugs of coffee.

"What if we want to stay?" he said. "We've all been looking forward to getting our own tasks finished. In fact, we're sort of committed. Very committed."

DeAvila shrugged. "That is your choice. It would be more helpful to us, of course, because a change of crew might be spotted and alert our smugglers - even though we've got a cover-story of you all coming down with a tummy bug to necessitate replacing you. You'll have to fake that, of course. If you stay on and go with the flow and pretend you don't know anything is amiss the chances are you won't come to any harm, but I'm afraid I'm not able to guarantee that. You're civilians and we can't ignore the dangers. If things did turn nasty the risks could be very real, and our people are trained to handle that sort of thing far better than you - no disrespect intended."

"How long can you give us to make our minds up?" asked Giles. "And what has she got to do with it?" he looked across at Zofia.

"This is all very confidential, of course, and whether you stay with us or go home nobody outside these walls should get wind of it, with the exception of Roger Percy and the Tiptons. But here's how the whole thing works, roughly of course: Zofia is one of our top agents, but so far as this operation is concerned she is on the run, a confidence trickster - it's getting too hot for her in France and she needs to 'disappear' among the Roma in Hungary. As a 'crooked' lorry driver, or rather co-driver, I've agreed to smuggle her there in our utility cabin, keeping her out of site of the rest of you ... a task I might say is becoming increasingly difficult. But for the moment it's important to go on as if she hasn't been sprung. Her language skills up ahead are going to be invaluable - she's a native speaker in several languages and dialects in that region."

"Including English!" the subject of DeAvila's discourse said, adding a deep, rich chuckle.

"But does this mean the whole bleeding business of the lorry being stolen was all prearranged, so that we could pick *her* up?" said Derek Jones, the light of realisation spreading over his face.

DeAvila nodded. "But I'm sorry, Derek, it even goes a good bit farther back than that. Do you remember those people I met near Liverpool? That was the first vital link in the game. They put the word out that I was to be trusted and just before we set off I was given a big wad of laundered drugs money to go back to Hungary. Nearly a million quid in big untraceable 1,000 Frank Swiss banknotes."

"What? You mean we're carrying that with us now?" Derek was again shocked.

De Avila nodded. "It's in the tank with the big fish. So now we've established two things with the Mafia or whoever is behind this - first, we have a set-up to take laundered money across borders, and

84

second, I'm prepared to do cash deals to smuggle people around too - that's where Zofia fits in. If in time I take over from Derek and do trips on my own, or with a co-driver of my own choice, I could be very valuable to them."

Zofia gave a little cough to interrupt this. "It's not the most comfortable travelling home I've had," she said. "But at least it's dry. And the nets are a bit fishy, but that's all to the good if it confuses any sniffer dogs at the borders."

"So what do we do ... wait until they try to get the money, then jump on them?" said Giles, switching his gaze between Moreau and DeAvila. At this, Moreau groaned and held his head in his hands. Then, pressing his knuckles into his eye sockets, he said emphatically: "No, no, no! Nobody is to jump on anybody. Anything at all like that you leave to us, do you understand? The whole idea is that you appear to be innocently unaware of anything underhand."

"Even if we're arrested for people-smuggling and money-laundering?" Giles pressed.

"Even so. If that was the case, we'd be able to get you off the hook anyway."

"I sincerely hope you're right. That means we have to trust you rather a lot."

The Frenchman nodded. In the silence that followed Giles's mobile phone rang. "My brother," he said to the rest and listened for a few minutes as Tipton told him about his own visitor.

"Yes, we know," said Giles when he had finished.

"Oh," said Tipton, sounding crestfallen at having his thunder stolen. "And are you as mad as I am about being hoodwinked like this?"

"Just a little," replied Giles.

"And are you all coming back?"

Giles looked around the faces in the room. "I wouldn't think so for one moment," he said. "Just like you, we see our missions through. Hang on a mo and I'll ask around." He raised his voice to address Mark, Derek and Mike. "Any of you want to go back?"

"No," said Mike, eagerly, "I'm in."

Derek leaned back in his chair and took a sip of coffee, lowered his cup. "I suppose that means I'm with you too. Besides, I bet none of the other MI5 blokes knows anything about looking after fish. Can we all get cracking soon - don't want to keep everyone waiting for their money, do we?"

Kendal merely shrugged, and said: "Yes, let's get on with it."

Giles said to his brother: "Does that answer your question?"

"Thought that might be the case," was Tipton's response.

Before ending the call he held the phone out to Mike.

"Somebody wants to speak to you."

It was Vicky. He struggled to stop himself blushing.

"Are you sure you want to do this?" Her voice was full of real concern. "What would your mother say?"

Turning away from his companions and doing his best to make his voice too soft to over hear, he said: "I'm OK. I think I'm old enough to look after myself."

"I know you are. But do be careful please."

"I will."

Of course they heard it all. Mark Kendal put a friendly arm around his shoulders.

"Don't worry, my boy, we'll all look after you, won't we?" He looked round at the others.

Mike lost his embarrassment in the laughter that followed. But he had a serious question for DeAvila. He'd promised his paper a running journal on what was happening along the trip. How much of these startling new developments could he reveal?

DeAvila looked him straight in the eye. "Nothing at all, if you don't mind - things get about more quickly than you realise these days. It could endanger not only the rest of this trip but future investigations too - and it would blow my cover of course. I'm afraid this is one case where free and fearless journalism has to be put to one side for all our sakes. I trust you can see that? But do send back reports of our progress, the scenery, that sort of thing ... anything that encourages the notion that everything is going smoothly with no monkey-business. Perhaps one day you'll be able to tell the true story - in your memoirs, maybe."

Mike nodded his assent. The meeting concluded with Moreau advising everyone to keep in touch through their mobile telephones, adding: "And call me if there is anything to report - anything at all, no matter how insignificant it might seem."

***

The only members of the Crimson Trout venture who knew nothing of this turn of events were the travelling fish, whose welfare could not be forgotten whatever external matters befell the whole operation. Derek, who knew his business thoroughly, kept up his regular tank inspections and water quality and temperature checks. In spite of the fact that the scaly voyagers were now encountering warmer weather, all appeared well. There was some feeding too for the smaller fish - just enough to keep them ticking over and no spare matter to fester and foul the tanks. Any droppings were filtered out. And Gobblemouth too was given his daily herring ration, appearing completely unperturbed by what must by now have seemed an endless journey in confinement.

Increasingly, Gobblemouth found people were talking to him: undoubtedly unintelligible noise to a fish, but nevertheless recognisably different depending on who was peering down at him after opening the lid of his plastic prison.

Derek was the most frequent of his visitors, usually greeting him with: "Hello, old boy - how are you doing today?"

Kendal was the most likely to deliver a fish, he found, often saying as he dropped in the food, "Well, I'm blowed - a tasty herring on the dinner menu for you mate. What a surprise!" or something similar.

Giles had a brief and businesslike: "All present and correct, are we? Well done."

Mike would usually say nothing while his head was in the opening, but would shout to the others while he withdrew it: "All OK!"

DeAvila, so far, had been most silent of them all, though he frequently leaned further into the tank so that he could see the inside of the top area and the package that had been secreted there.

And lately, there had been a new face and a new voice, a woman. So far she had only said: "Wow - that is one big fish!"

If he had a long memory he might have connected that voice with his distant past, and if he had been able to reason (and who is to say he couldn't?) he might have wondered what sort of coincidence had led him to hear it again.

***

There was a very different atmosphere as they headed out on the road once again.

In deference to Zofia's mild complaint about the effect his fishy nets were having on her feminine allure, Derek had taken them from the cabin temporarily and roped them down between the fish tanks. This left her the sweeter-smelling tarpaulins on which to lay out her sleeping bag. He even filled his own vacuum flask with coffee for her.

However, the fact that their adventure had taken on a darker and more dangerous tone could not be avoided, try as they might to make everything appear as normal as possible.

"Suddenly, we're all secret agents," Kendal said to Mike. "Do you think there's a job in this? Will they sign us up for MI5? I always fancied myself as James Bond."

"Shush," said Mike. "They've probably got a satellite listening in to us." Then he got a laugh from Kendal when he suggested: "But it's tempting to think of Moreau as 'Mother', isn't it?"

Like everyone else, Mike was increasingly nervous - and excited - as they neared the border with Italy. Checking over the papers he might need, he told Kendal it would soon be time for him to take DeAvila's place in the truck while they entered a new country.

They had been told by Moreau that there would probably be little bother during this event: he'd prepared the way with border authorities. What would be more interesting would be seeing what happened once they were well inside Italy, and Moreau warned them to be prepared for an unscheduled stop, something DeAvila had previously arranged with his criminal 'pals', so that the smugglers, or rather their agents, could check that all was going to plan. But although DeAvila knew this meeting was going to happen, he had not been told exactly where or when.

"Borders are not a great problem: all the countries we go through, except Croatia, are in the Schengen zone," Mike informed Kendal.

"Schengen? What the hell's that?"

"An open borders agreement. It's named after the place they signed the treaty. All a bit iffy since we decided to quit the EU."

"You don't say. Sounds Chinese."

"It's actually named after a place in Luxembourg."

***

Although everyone was as tense as an over-wound guitar string, crossing the border proved to be an anti-climax as predicted; the Range Rover and the campervan were waved through, and the papers that Mike offered through the fish transporter truck's window were given a cursory glance before it too was freed. They drew in immediately for Mike and DeAvila to once again change places. Mike was not surprised to see Moreau's car also parked near the Italian border buildings, though there was no sign of the little man.

With a lot of the earlier tension now released, Giles suggested they should try to keep in convoy, with the Range Rover leading and the campervan bringing up the rear, and they set off again on a fast stretch of road that started to rapidly eat up miles. All appeared well and they held formation until, about 15 miles into the new country, Mike was dismayed to see the Range Rover pulling up on the hard shoulder, its hazard lights flashing, as they sped on past.

"Looks like they've got a puncture,". he said to Kendal. "What do we do? We can't turn around."

As ever resourceful, Kendal said: "Contact them by mobile - Derek or DeAvila first, to tell them to stop at the earliest opportunity, a petrol station or roadside rest but not a motorway exit, then phone Giles to find out what's happened and to tell him we'll be waiting. If he can't fix the tyre himself, it shouldn't take too long for a breakdown service to reach him. Hopefully, anyhow."

Mike called Derek, who answered: "Right - we'll keep our eyes skinned for a suitable stop." Giles, as Mike surmised, had indeed suffered a puncture. An Australian, he was adept at changing over to the spare wheel alone in outback situations so changing it by the side of a motorway was "hairy, but OK". In all he reckoned he would lose only twenty minutes at most, even though it had started raining. Mike and Kendal plugged on in the lorry's wake under darkening skies.

"Hey, watch it!"

It was only when Kendal's voice rang out that Mike realised his sleepiness, and he snapped fully awake to see a large dark van cutting in between them and the fish truck. Kendal had the heel of his hand hard down on the horn but nevertheless the vehicle nudged in.

"Italian drivers!" Kendal was annoyed. But he was even more annoyed a minute later when the fish truck again veered violently and he saw it peeling away to the right on a slip road, sandwiched between the van and a large dark car with an official-looking flashing blue light on top.

"Damn, damn, damn!" he spluttered. "We've been cut out. They've been hijacked!"

They stopped five miles later at a petrol station, crestfallen. Mike tried to telephone Giles or Derek and DeAvila, but nobody answered.

"I expect they're busy right now," said Kendal. "In fact, calling Jones and DeAvila right now might be a complication too far. And we can't very well go back and follow them, not immediately anyway - we could upset the whole plan. Let's go in for a coffee and hope for the best. I think it's all we can do."

Chapter 9

There was no mistaking the message the uniformed man in the back of the car ahead was signalling by jabbing his finger: pull off, turn right. Derek Jones had little choice but to comply. "What the f**k do they want?" he said, irritated, to Pedro DeAvila, noticing at the same time that a large vehicle had managed to insert itself between the truck and Kendal's following campervan speeding off along the highway.

DeAvila shrugged, and said something that brought a chill: "I doubt they're real policemen."

Cutting them out and sending them peeling away from the motorway had been executed with efficiency and now they were being escorted along a rough-surfaced works access track sandwiched between the two vehicles. To stop would mean a minor accident at least.

"Is this it, do you think?"

"It's something, that's for sure," said DeAvila tersely. "Keep calm and carry on is the motto, I think - so far as we're concerned it's just an official police check. I'm sure that's what they'll want us to think. But just in case, pretend you haven't seen this..."

Reaching into an inner pocket of his bomber jacket, he drew out a blue metal handgun, clicked its magazine into place and repocketed it. Derek Jones tensed - was this really happening, he asked himself? Just how much danger had he let himself in for?

DeAvila reached over and patted him reassuringly on the shoulder.

"Relax. We'll all be fine."

"Bollocks we will."

They entered a large, flat open area with mountains of gravel and sand at its edges - a roadmender's depot. The only building was a small wooden shed beside which was parked a yellow bulldozer and an old red tractor with a scoop bucket. Still sandwiched, they were pulled up beside this. Three uniformed but hatless men climbed out of the car and one of them came back to the truck cab. The driver of the van stayed in his vehicle. Derek wound down his window. A piece of paper was waved briefly at him and just as quickly pocketed again.

"Customs check," the man said. "Stay in seats please. It will take minutes, no more. Then you can go on your way again."

He was a tall man, dark and well-muscled, but Derek was more than relieved the words did not seem threatening. His henchmen moved to the back of the truck and Derek and DeAvila felt the vibrations as they clambered aboard. Derek's main concern was for Zofia - apart from anything else it would be a big shock for her to have the door of the tackle cubby opened by strangers. And what would they do with her when they found her?

"Is anything locked?" said their inquisitor.

"Nothing. Just the toolbox. Do you want the key?"

Derek singled out the right one on his keyring and started to hand it to the man but he waved it away.

"No. Not necessary."

Even as he said this his companions were jumping down from the truck bed and making their way back to the car. They did not have Zofia with them, Derek was glad to see. In fact, come to think of it, he hadn't even heard the door of the cubby being opened.

"That is all, thank you. Now you can follow us to the track in the top left of the yard. Turn left and It will lead you back onto the autostrada."

As promised, the hit had been quick. The two vehicles that had brought them off course were driven swiftly away and were out of sight before the truck reached the track: soon, as promised, they were buzzing along the motorway again, looking out for any likely places the campervan and the Range Rover might be waiting for them.

***

Pulling into the first petrol station they came to, they were relieved to see the campervan. It was empty. They were about to get out of the truck and make their way to the cafe area when DeAvila said: "You go ahead. I'll hang back and check Zofia's all right. We might be being watched still, so it's time for me to look furtive again. I'll check the fish are OK too."

In the cafe Jones found a relieved Mike and Kendal who told them Giles was on his way after fitting his spare wheel. He was sitting down with a coffee when an ashen-faced DeAvila reappeared.

"Zofia?" Jones said anxiously.

"No, no - she's fine. And so are the fish. It's the money - it isn't in the tank anymore. It must have been taken and there isn't a sign they've left anything in return."

***

Giles was just as shocked as the rest of them when he arrived around twenty minutes later.

"What do we do now? Pedro, you know more than the rest of us about this - how do you read the situation? Do you think the money was supposed to be picked up at this point, or is there some double-dealing going on?"

DeAvila shrugged. "I really don't know. If they stole it for themselves, working outside the master plan, we're in trouble, I guess."

"So what do we do?" Giles repeated. "Still pretend we don't know anything, right?"

DeAvila smiled at the irony in Giles' voice. "We pretty much have to, don't we? Look, whatever happens it's a matter between the smugglers and the people who just stopped us. Keep that in mind - and try not to worry."

"Worry? We've just been robbed of a million bloody quid and the man tells us not to worry! I'm glad it's all OK then."

The fresh irony came from Derek Jones. DeAvila gave him a reassuring grin, then looked round the others and said: "I've got good reason to say that. You really shouldn't know this, because the less you know the better for all concerned and you in particular. But there is some contingency back-up."

"What sort of backup?" said Giles.

"Cash. For safety's sake my lords and masters provided a duplicate package with the same amount of money. It's safely hidden in the metal tool locker and so far as I can see that hasn't been tampered with. They knew where they should be looking for the money and they went straight to the fish tank."

The relief was visible on their faces, but Giles had a further question.

"Why didn't they do anything about Zofia?"

"If picking up the money at this stage was really part of their plan - and we've no real reason yet to suspect that it wasn't - then I expect they wouldn't want to draw attention to her presence in the cubby. If Derek had heard a woman's voice back there he might have been very surprised and would want to investigate - catching them in the act of removing the money."

"Well, thanks for telling us all this at least," said Giles. "I don't suppose you can also tell us what other nasty little surprises might wait for us from here on in, can you?"

He earned a level look and a characteristic DeAvila shrug. "Your guess is as good as mine. But well done, everyone, for keeping your cool. And thanks."

***

As the youngest and certainly the least travelled of the group, Mike Cook found the next stage of the trip across the north of Italy a novel and fascinating experience. Although they were moving on fast roads there was plenty to see, especially the occasional glimpses of the mountains which were always in and out of view. He tried to put the money incident to the back of his mind but he was aware that it had cast a long shadow across the venture. Passing exit signs pointing to cities like Turin and Milan, however, helped him to forget their ever-present dangers. They had a memorable meal by the shores of Lake Garda (DeAvila making a credible show of smuggling food to Zofia in her stuffy prison) and by the end of the day's travel they were well past Verona and getting close to their next border crossing. Giles and Derek Jones' overnight hotel had a wireless link which gave Mike an opportunity to email Vicky with news of their progress, although DeAvila had sworn everyone to secrecy about the brief lorry hijack and the disappearance of the money. Indeed, did Vicky know anything at all about the amount of money, he wondered? He was also able to send a sanitised trip blog back to his paper, with some digital camera pictures he had taken. And a cheery message to his mum, of course omitting details of the recent drama.

Vicky sent a long email in return: greetings and continuing good luck to everyone from Tipton (plus an anxious note from him for a report on the wellbeing of the fish, particularly Gobblemouth). She conveyed a brief message from Mike's mum too, saying all was well back at home. Finally, she wrote: 'Love from Vicky, X'. He found that particularly pleasing. After sending a reply back to be passed on to to his mother that he was keeping well and looking forward to the next stage of the adventure, and another to Tipton reporting that the fish were fine, he hesitated briefly, then wrote: 'Thanks Vicky. Love from me too, X', closed the machine down and made his way happily back to the campervan and another night of Kendal's awful snores.

Even though he had become almost immune to the night-time racket, this time Mike failed to drop off for more than moments at a time. Mainly this was because he knew that the conclusion of the outward run was now getting very close, and along with that there had to be a resolution of some sort to the smuggling situation, and the dangers this posed. And more than once or twice he asked himself if he had been too forward in signing off with 'love' to Vicky.

His other worry was that if he didn't get at least some sleep he might feel wretched for the rest of the next day. But towards dawn he dropped off for a longer period of deep sleep, and when he woke he felt ready for anything.

***

Mike and Kendal heard raised voices coming from the hotel terrace table where DeAvila, Derek Jones and Giles were waiting to start the morning briefing. All was not well. As they approached the argument broke off.

"Something the matter?" asked Kendal cautiously as he sat down. Mike hovered, unsure, until Giles gestured he should sit down too. "Not a big problem, I hope. A little bit complicated - I'll try to keep it brief. Derek here found two dead trout in the tanks this morning, and he's worried. There's nothing wrong with the water quality or anything, or the temperature - he thinks it's travel stress. Can't say I'd like to travel all this way in a plastic tank slopping all over the place. Derek thinks we should try to find a suitable water or a fish farm with spare capacity to offload them as quick as we can - he knows one or two candidates for this or we could make a dash back for the south of France where we made the last drop. But the change of plan would upset our smugglers. That's Pedro's side of the dilemma - and we are supposed to be getting Zofia into Croatia, which is also where the cash exchange was planned to take place: a

97

million or so in Swiss Francs in exchange for a package of other currencies ready to go to the laundry. I think that's about the size of it, isn't it?"

"Wait a moment - haven't you forgotten Gobblemouth?" Mike cut in, hiding a pang of disappointment and deeply concerned about suddenly losing the purpose of their mission.

"No of course we haven't forgotten him. It's not so difficult, apparently. For some time now we've been driving along the River Po valley, and it's chokka with big catfish, according to the internet. We could slip him in unnoticed, I'm sure," said Giles. "Is that right?" he said, appealing to Kendal as the big fish expert. Kendal nodded.

The two who had been arguing the toss looked at each other. Derek Jones spoke first.

"It's really difficult, you know. I always put the welfare of my fish first. I think most of you would do the same, wouldn't you? I hope you would. And it wouldn't be any bloody good driving around with a load of dead fish, would it? I mean, who's that going to fool?"

DeAvila grimaced. "Under normal circumstances, yes, I'd agree with you one hundred per cent. But there's more to breaking up this particular ring than meets the eye. The money either represents drugs, which bring untold misery with them, or destroyed lives if smuggled people get dumped in the middle of nowhere or, worse, killed once the money is handed over. And some of the money could go to some of the nastier radical elements in the Middle East. These people don't think much of their fellow human beings, as you know. In any event the cost of the fish will be compensated if they are lost."

Giles coughed politely to interrupt. "I can see where both of you are coming from. On balance though, I'm sorry to say I put people ahead of the fish, Derek. Would it help if I rang your boss to see what he thinks? If we do things DeAvila's way and stick to the original plan we'll only have to worry about the fish for another day and a bit, after all."

Derek Jones thought a moment then nodded, avoiding DeAvila's eyes, clearly still not entirely convinced. Giles took out his mobile phone, put it on the table and tapped out the number.

"I hope they're all awake," he said. It took a little while for the call to go through, but when Giles eventually spoke, his first two words brought a sudden knot to Mike Cook's stomach.

"Hello Vicky. Hope all's well, but we'd like a quick word with Roger Percy. Can you put us through - it's quite important."

There was a pause, and then he said, "OK" and put the phone down before looking round the expectant faces.

"She said she'd get him to call as soon as she could find him - he's 'somewhere in the works', which sounds a little painful to me. I suggest we all get ready to move off as soon as we hear from him."

"We're set already," said Kendal.

"Me too," said Giles.

Derek looked at DeAvila. "Come along. We'll get the engine warmed up," he said, and to Giles: "You'd better bring the phone over too."

When the call did come through Derek spent some time speaking to Roger Percy while the others gathered around his cab.

"All right then," he said eventually. "I understand. I'll tell the rest. Goodbye." Addressing himself mainly to DeAvila he said: "We go your way. But if there's an increasing problem with the fish we get them to the nearest clean-looking river or stream and let them go, whether or not we're breaking the law: he says he's been assured the government will get us out of any trouble we find ourselves in. I'm happy with that."

Kendal felt a twinge of concern. "Do we let Gobblemouth go too?"

"I guess so," said Derek, who at that moment was wishing he could be anywhere else. He added briskly: "Let's get going, shall we? I think we've been hanging around here long enough. It's a bloody 'orrible place. And I'll do my best to keep all our little friends alive."

***

Venice was signposted off to the right as the little convoy sped ever closer to the Slovenian border. A bit later the next boundary crossing again went without a hitch - just some cursory paper-checking for the lorry - and once again, Mike spotted Moreau's little car parked outside one of the deserted-looking border control buildings.

The young man felt a thrill moving into this new country. Reading strange-sounding place names was like leaving the familiarity of near-Europe behind and plunging into the unknown. Within the day, he knew, they would be across yet another border, and it was one that meant the climax of the dangerous part of the mission that had been wished upon them. Although it was hard to look beyond this anticipated event, the end of the day would, with luck, see them also getting close to the Danube with their two original objectives in sight: the delivery of Gobblemouth to his original home, and the fairytale-like search for crimson trout. Even without the strangeness of the new country they had entered, it was hard to fight back the excitement continually bubbling up in his stomach - increasingly so with each minute that passed .

They passed Ljubjana and pressed on, and when he got a call from Giles to say everyone was pulling in at a place called Maribor for a final briefing, Mike had to make a big effort to calm himself down.

"Are you feeling OK?" Kendal asked, concerned, as they left the main road, though he had much the same feelings himself. Mike nodded. They were not at all surprised to see that Moreau's car was also parked at the impromptu layby stop, with the Frenchman and DeAvila in a huddle while Giles and Derek Jones looked on with their hands on their hips, unable to understand much of what was being said.

It was a bleak spot: the layby overlooked a deep, craggy wooded ravine with glimpses of a torrent far below. High above circled large birds of prey, and their harsh calls could be heard drifting down once the engines were switched off.

Up on the truck bed, the cubby door was slightly ajar so that Zofia could be party to the proceedings without making an appearance that could be noticed from any passing vehicle. The huddle broke up as they joined the group and DeAvila addressed them all.

"Thanks, all," he said. "We're all very pleased with how you've handled things so far, but we thought it was only right to offer you another chance to step aside after the border while we take over - we can hand things back to you once the money exchange has taken place and you can carry on as if nothing ever happened. What do you all think?"

"I think I'm staying on for the duration," Giles said at once. "How about you, Kendal? Mike?"

They looked at each other.

"I think we're in too," said Kendal.

A sudden ethereal call came from behind the cubby door, accented and mocking: "I do like the British spirit. Well done, all of you. But I wish you'd make this cabin a little more comfortable. I do want to be delivered alive." It was followed by a chuckle which made everyone smile.

DeAvila's look became serious. "So far as we know, the Croatian boys have been double-crossed by the Mafia in Italy, and they'll be furious if they don't find any money. We're playing plan B and replacing the money in the hope they don't suspect anything at all yet. By the way, Moreau told me the gang that kidnapped you only got as far as Bologna before they were intercepted by our Italian colleagues, and nearly all the cash has been recovered. By all accounts they were a breakaway group doing a double sting. But I'm afraid it does mean a rumour underground that something fishy is going on, so if that news has reached Croatia ahead of us things might not be so easy as we thought. You'll have to take my word for it, but we've got an armed team waiting in the wings if things do get at all rough. If that influences the way you think about the affair, there's still time to back out."

Heads were being shaken all around. He went on: "Good. What I can promise you is that we'll try our best not do anything to put you in danger while the handover goes through, or even after it for that matter - all we are interested in is detecting all the people involved and mapping out the network. We wouldn't have done it any other way, for your sakes especially. No do-or-die heroics from you, mind. Just play it cool."

If it was meant to calm things down, it didn't pour any cold water at all on Mike's excitement.

Before the group broke up DeAvila produced a wallet and a mobile phone from his grip in the truck cab and passed it to Derek Jones.

"You'll need this."

"What is it?" said Derek, gingerly opening the wallet. "There's money in here. And bank cards, health card, a driving licence..."

"A substitute for your own money and phone, for the time being - give your wallet to Giles for safe keeping. It's all part of the plan. I'll explain later. In the meantime, can everyone please copy Derek's new number on their own phones."

***

Another uneventful crossing and several miles of plain sailing along pleasant roads left Mike wondering if he had been dreaming about the darker nature their trip had take on. Bit by bit the anticipation lessened of a sudden interruption and frenzied action to follow. He scarcely noticed a roadworks sign and the diversion notice which Kendal followed. The route they now took was smaller but even more likeable than the one they had left. Parts of it seemed very similar to an English country lane: even the wayside plants and overblown flowers of late summer looked familiar. An exclamation from Kendal followed by abrupt braking brought him to full alert.

"What?"

"That's the main road ahead of us again. I think we've been sent round in a circle - this is just where we left it. Give Derek Jones a call on his new phone, will you? Might be nothing but I think there's something odd going on. I'll try to turn us round and pull up somewhere safe."

While Kendal struggled to get the big vehicle round with a seven or eight point turn, Mike listened to the constant unanswered ring tone from Derek's substitute phone until the message service cut in. DeAvila's phone was also unanswered.

"Try Giles," Kendal suggested.

Giles answered with one word, "Hold." A moment later he said: "There, I'm off the road. What's happened?"

"Are you OK?" Mike asked. "Did you take the diversion?"

"Diversion? What diversion?"

It was becoming clear that the fish truck had been cleverly separated once again from Giles and themselves. Giles, who had seen no diversion signs at all, was now some way ahead along the main road.

"Ask him to wait," said Kendal. "If he meets any one while he's poking around these lanes they might take a pot-shot at him. I've a hunch our truck's somewhere in this area. I'm going round the block again. Keep your eyes peeled for side-tracks, farmyards, that sort of thing. Or they could be in a field. And if any trouble does come up, young Cook, keep well out of the way, do you hear me? I don't want to have to explain to your mum how I let you blunder blindly into danger."

103

Mike was on the edge of his seat as they retraced their steps. Kendal drew up at a junction were there had been a diversion sign before: It was now missing.

"I wonder..." he said, turning the van to take the opposite direction to the one that had directed them in a circle.

***

They did not have far to go: the tail of the fish truck appeared inside an open gateway leading into a cobbled quadrangle surrounded by low iron-roofed barns, some of them open-fronted. Kendal backed the van up the lane to get a better view through the gateway, pulled up and put his handbrake on. There were no other vehicles in the yard; in fact the whole scene looked deserted - including the truck cab. The door of the cubby was wide open, too, and Zofia was obviously not inside.

"Wait," said Kendal, "and if that sounds like an order, it is."

Leaving the engine running for a swift getaway he opened his door and dropped quietly to the ground, then entered the courtyard cautiously, looking nervously all about him. Mike felt a pang of fear: What if anything happened to Kendal - what would he do? Drive away on his own? What if they - whoever 'they' were - came after him? Involuntarily he clenched his fists tightly, his fingernails digging into his palms.

He watched with rising tension as Kendal crept towards the front of the lorry,, stopping to listen for a moment then standing on its cab step to reach for the door handle. Gently he pulled the door wide open. Nobody. He stepped down, listened again briefly, and then called: "Hello - anyone there? Derek? Pablo?"

Nothing. Kendal signalled Mike to switch off the van engine and join him. The yard was baking hot, still and very, very quiet.

"No sign of them."

"What now?"

"We'd better search these buildings for them first. Let's hope they're still alive, wherever they are."

Kendal's words brought Mike a new chill: what if they now discovered bodies? What if they never saw the two ever again? What had happened to Zofia? Suddenly he felt a long, long way from home, and, apart from Kendal, utterly alone.

"You start from that side and I'll go this way round," Kendal directed, businesslike.

"What about the fish - are they still there? And the money?" said Mike, with sudden concern.

"Blow the bloody fish," said Kendal. "Let's get on with it, eh?"

Mike jumped as he flushed a just as startled barn-owl out of the first of the open buildings and was about to enter the second when a shout from Kendal stopped him.

"Over here! Quick!"

Mike found Kendal untying a very much alive bound and gagged Derek Jones; another bound figure in the corner was just kicking himself up into sitting position against a stack of straw bales and Mike hurried over to help free DeAvila.

"Thanks," DeAvila said when Mike untied the loose gag. "What kept you two?"

***

Just like Mike and Kendal, Derek Jones and Pedro DeAvila had steered off the road to follow diversion signs. DeAvila had been a little more wary than Kendal about the authenticity of the temporary road signs.

"Let's be careful now," he said to Derek, "This could well be the moment. But remember you're supposed to think that I'm not part of the plot, even though the gang believe I'm on their side. They want to keep us and this rig as a nice little earner for the future, with you unwittingly ferrying money and more back and forth. My info is they'll try to make it look like an unsophisticated highway robbery to get our phones and our wallets, which is why we've done the switch back down the road. They'll get the phones and the bit of cash we put in the wallets but they'll find the fake bank card blocked and they'll get gobbled up by cash machines if they try to use them. They get the pay-dirt cash in the tank, of course, and somewhere along the road back we'll pick up another laundering package. They'll tie us up but the deal is they leave me able to get free without too much trouble. They'll take Zofia of course - she'll be freed in the next town."

"I'm OK," said Derek, looking around warily as they drove along the narrowing lane. "But I can't pretend I'm looking forward to it. And what will they do when they find the credit cards don't work?"

DeAvila shrugged. "Not a worry - it's not really what they're after and they'll just think we managed to get the cards cancelled."

Another diversion sign at a fork in the road took them left and Derek had the impression that they were steadily moving into deeper country away from the main road. Suddenly a man stepped out into the middle of the lane, a shotgun held across his chest. Taking one hand off the weapon he pointed to an open roadside gateway beside a group of agricultural buildings.

"Here we bloody well go again," said Derek with a quaver in his voice. "I hope they're reading all this from your script and not a completely different one."

DeAvila put a steadying hand on his shoulder and he stopped the truck in front of three more armed men leaning against a large, black four-wheel-drive. One of the men moved to Derek's side of the truck cab and gestured for him to open it and step down while another went to DeAvila's door.

Derek wondered if they could see his knees trembling as he was searched. He certainly felt no urge to challenge the process with so many weapons around. The leader had very few words and did not

106

say anything Derek could comprehend before he was marched into one of the buildings and tied up hand and foot while sitting on a square straw bale. They weren't rough with him but neither were they at all timid. Then they gagged him - by far the most unpleasant experience so far - and left him. As they walked unhurriedly out he saw that one of them was carrying his erstwhile 'new' wallet in one hand and another was clicking away on the substitute phone.

***

"And that was about that so far as all the drama and excitement was concerned," Derek told Mike and Kendal. "Not that I'm not glad to see you both. Theoretically Pedro was only loosely tied but it was taking him a mighty long time to get free."

Now that the much-anticipated action was over, Mike felt disappointment. It seemed an anti-climax even though it made a good story - one that he might one day write up, perhaps changing names and circumstances so that - heeding DeAvila's warnings - any ongoing investigations into the serious business of people-smuggling and money-laundering would not be jeopardised.

"I suppose we're out of danger now?" Mike ventured.

DeAvila shuffled his feet, looking down. "Er..I'm afraid not. Not altogether, anyway - so long as I'm part of the crew this is a marked lorry, so to speak, and the underworld is quite a sophisticated network where news travels fast. I've got Roger Percy's agreement to stay aboard if the rest of you go along with that, but if you have misgivings let me know and we'll engineer a row or something to let you off the hook. The word is round that I will do anything for a buck or two and I can expect more approaches. Might not happen of course but if it does I will try to keep you all informed. And by the way, I've agreed to take Zofia on to Hungary with us provided I can sweet-talk Derek here into picking her up as a hitch-hiker further along the road. Does anyone have any objections to all of that?"

Derek Jones rubbed his chafed wrists ruefully, but grinned. "In for a penny, in for a pound," he said. "Shall we check the fish are all right and get on with it? We're going to be late for our final delivery as it is."

Besides all that, Mike reminded himself, there was still the Quest for the Crimson Trout to be accomplished, not to mention the return of Gobblemouth to his roots. Somehow neither of these events had quite the same ring of excitement about them after what they had just been through. But there was always the chance he might be proved wrong.

Chapter 10

"Quick - Pedro, switch on that bloody aerator right away!"

There was urgency and anger in Derek Jones' voice: their attackers had shut down everything on the lorry, including the life-support systems for the fish. Many of the already travel-stressed trout were at the surface gasping for air, and some had even turned on their sides - sure signs they were at the edge of survival.

Even with the vital connections restored Derek point blank refused to move the fish until all appeared to be on the mend. It was two hours before everyone was reunited with Giles to tell him their tale.

"Fair Dinkum?" he said. "I'm real sorry I missed all that!"

It sounded like he actually meant it.

Back on the road, just after they had passed a small town, a lone figure was flagging down the transporter: they pulled in and Zofia clambered aboard, this time sitting between Derek and DeAvila, once more part of the quest. "I will still sleep with your beautifully-perfumed nets," she informed them. "I am used to them by now. And I find it ... amusing."

When they next gathered for a roadside briefing to make sure everyone was headed for the right place, Giles insisted Zofia had a more comfortable ride in the Range Rover with him. But he couldn't get her to change her mind about sleeping on the truck - his offer to payroll a B&B was waved airily away.

"But you're alone out there. What if somebody breaks into the cubby?"

"I tell you, I can scream very, very loud. Best burglar alarm you ever had. Do you want to hear?"

She drew a deep breath to oblige, but Giles's gestures made it quite clear he would take her word for it.

***

The afternoon was well advanced as they neared the final drop for their trout. Phoning ahead, they had made sure people would be there to meet them, but as it was a straight-into-the-water job it would not take very long: chutes would be opened up in the tank sides with the lorry parked right at the water's edge.

"Oh!"

Mike let out a gasp of surprise. Increasingly the terrain around them had become rocky and wooded, but the landscape they had just burst through into was little short of magical. To either side of the road lay pool after pool of crystal clear water, each connected to one another by curtain-like waterfalls.

"Now that's something you don't see every day," Kendal observed, just as gobsmacked. "I've heard Croatia is beautiful, but this is something else. It's a national park centred on Papuk mountain - not quite so well-known as Plitvice, apparently, but then again you can have too many tourists, can't you?"

And it was into waters like this, they soon learned, that their much-travelled French trout were to be delivered - some for a pool to supply local restaurants enjoying an increasing tourist trade, and some actually into river-linked pools where it was hoped they might breed and populate the region, conditions being similar to rivers on America's west coast where rainbow trout originated.

Eventually they watched the last of the fish make their way into the darkening waters and the beds of brilliant green weed still glowing in the dwindling light.

"Don't you have any trout of your own?" Kendal said to one of their Croatian helpers, half-joking. "I'd have thought this was ideal for them."

The man's stubbly face broke into a broad grin.

"Oh yes - we did have plenty of brown trouts just here. Then somebody brought along fish you call pikes I think. Suddenly, no more trouts."

Though Kendal was surprised that pike were an introduced fish to this particular chain of pools, he knew all about the dangers of moving species around without any thought for the consequences - especially predatory pike. Yet here they were introducing rainbow trout, which seemed to fly in the face of caution. He could only hope the exercise would not lead to more environmental disasters.

"I see," he said. "I'm sorry." He hoped the thoughtless pike-lover had not been an Englishman. But considering their drive in the area had now and then taken them not far from Croatia's River Drava, where Kendal knew there was good pike and zander fishing, it seemed more than likely that a local had transferred them. This was well off the beaten track for most English fishermen, though he had heard that more and more adventurous foreign anglers were discovering the region's treasures.

Quick to catch Kendal's frown the man slapped him reassuringly on the shoulder. "No, do not worry, we still have our big trouts in many lakes. This is just experiment to get eating fish locally. The big trouts too big to get on plates.

"How big?"

"Maybe twenty, twenty-five."

Kendal whistled. "Twenty-five pounds you mean."

"No - twenty-five *kilos*."

Well might he whistle - if that was true, these local trout were bigger than most pike!

***

Two of the men who had helped them unload came to the inn where they ate that night, late, and where Giles had a room. Mike was aware he'd probably had rather a lot of drink by the time the meal was finished but it was an exciting evening and local musicians who turned up in the bar were determined to entertain their guests, so whenever his glass was refilled he felt he could not refuse. Zofia also added to the buzz by performing a spirited dance with some of the inhabitants - she seemed glad she no longer had to stay under cover, and glad also she was among people whose language and customs she knew.

"Whoa!" Kendal exclaimed as she reeled giddily off the floor, hot and glowing, and plonked herself on the bench seat between him and Mike.

"Your turn now?" she said to Kendal, her eyes sparkling, and he held up his hands in protest.

"Me? No - my dancing days are over, I fear. I'm an old man. Take Mike."

And she did, for two more dances, bringing him back flushed and perspiring.

Everyone laughed. Then one of their new companions leaned across the wooden table top and asked seriously: " The big fish you still have, tell me - what is to become of him? Is he for food? We do not eat such fish here. They do not taste so good."

Kendal told them the story of Gobblemouth's discovery and their plan to return him to his origins. The Croatians raised their eyebrows.

"I was told the British are mad," one commented.

"Not so mad as Croatians," Zofia said, rising to the defence of her companions, and there followed an intense discussion of local politics during which Mike, Derek Jones and Giles were given a potted history of all the ills that had befallen the Balkans in recent times: it was, they were told, part of the continuing collapse of the Ottoman empire.

"I never knew it was so big, or so recent," said Kendal at one point, genuinely surprised.

"Oh yes. Under Suleiman the Great in the sixteenth century it stretched right through the Middle East and along the Mediterranean shore of North Africa, up to the Russian border, and in Europe right to the gates of Vienna. As you can see, it has been an Islam-inspired empire, and it remains an unsolved problem to this day. Hopefully sometime we can all live in peace, but there are long memories - and still plenty of hotheads. It is very difficult."

"Amen to that - the peace, I mean," said DeAvila, who was the only one among them, apart from Zofia, who seemed au fait with all this.

Sensing a need to change the subject before politics took over everything, Giles stepped in with: "This is a beautiful area and you're lucky to live here. Are there local foods we should be trying?"

They had already eaten a spicy fish stew, which the locals assured him could be found right up to the border where they would head for the next day.

"Okay," said Giles. "I'm happy to have more of that. Tell me, has anyone round here heard of crimson trout? Crimson is a colour - bright red. A bit like Zofia's shirt."

Heads were wagged, but one man said: "Somewhere in these mountains, maybe - there were lots of different sorts of trout before the pike came. I will find out for you if I can. You want to catch some, eat some?"

"We'll buy some if you can find any," said Giles, setting the bait. "If you can get some alive so much the better. We can call back this way in a couple of days. I'll give you a phone number to keep in touch."

113

***

Mike had suffered his share of hangovers before but nothing like the one he woke with. His first conscious moments were disconcerting: he was in a hotel bed with no memory how he happened to be there. However, there was another rumpled bed in the room and sounds were coming from the bathroom. He tried to sit up but fell back, his head swimming. Moments later Giles appeared in the bathroom door.

"Hey, how are you? If it's anything like me, it won't be too great. I think we hit it some."

Mike eased himself a little higher, bunching the pillow under his throbbing head. He was still fully dressed apart from his shoes. A snort from an easy chair in the corner of the room made him look round: scrunched up in it was Derek Jones wrapped in a quilt, apparently having a bit of trouble trying to open one eye. Mike looked back at Giles.

"How did I get here?"

"You walked. Or rather, you staggered, with a bit of help. Don't remember, eh...no, no, don't try to shake your head. It could fall off. Take a shower - it'll help!"

"Hell and bugger everything!" Grey-faced Derek raised his tousled head and muttered from his corner, "even my bloody blood hurts."

***

When they all eventually gathered round the breakfast table, a neat white lace tablecloth, toast and jam and jugs of coffee replacing the glasses and empty bottles of the night before, Giles observed: "The main thing to remember about hangovers is that things can only get better."

"Thanks awfully for that, old chap" Derek rejoined in a mock-posh voice.

Zofia was last to appear - she too had been found a vacant guest room, in spite of protests, as had Pedro DeAvila; Kendal had spent a reclusive night in his campervan. Although Zofia had been the one to enjoy the evening the most she seemed as fresh as a daisy, bright and cheerful.

After a couple of mugs of strong coffee Derek asked DeAvila if he had checked Gobblemouth.

"The big fellow seems all right," he said. "The water's a bit murky."

"Then we'll change it for him before we move off. After we've come so far It would be really silly to have a sick fish on our hands. I'll get a testing kit out but I think the water's pure enough here for human beings, let alone fish. Still, we don't want to take any chances, do we?"

The thought crossed Mike's mind that they were used to taking bigger chances by now.

With packed lunches from the guest house they were on the road again just before noon. Within a few miles, as they drifted down from the mountain with its idyllic scenery, Mike was sound asleep. He was jolted awake when Kendal almost ran the campervan into the back of the fish truck. It had one rear wheel in the ditch and was being surveyed by a worried Derek Jones. Kendal passed the lorry and found a field gateway to park in a little further up the road.

"The tail has been wagging a bit with all the weight back here," Derek told them when they joined him. "We just skipped sideways on the loose gravel on the bend. I should have kept some water in the other tanks instead of draining them. Can't quite see how we're going to get it out - the ditch is bloody deep and the bank and verge are soft. I phoned Giles and he's on his way back here."

***

115

Fortunately the road was not a busy one, and some of the drivers who did come along stopped to offer help when they realised the predicament. DeAvila was able to converse with some amount of ease, but nobody was carrying the sort of stout planks that would provide an instant solution. When Giles and Zofia reappeared, it was decided to build a small ramp infilling the ditch so that the cab tractor that drove the rig could pull the trapped back wheel up and out - with luck. Any stones, logs and dried lumps of mud that could be found at the roadside were gathered and hauled back to make the ramps.

But when they had finished the construction Derek still tut-tutted about its suitability.

"The ground's still very soft under it all," he complained. "Too soft to my mind. I'm worried it will sink again. And this time all that muck will be around it to make things worse. I'm afraid we're just too back-heavy."

Giles was about to ask if the driver was not being too over-cautious, but Derek's deep frown made him hold his tongue, in that respect at least. Instead he said: "I've got a towing cable in the car - what if I link up to the front of your truck for extra pulling power? If we're quick we might get it out before the ramp gives way."

But Derek was still not happy. "What might make some difference is emptying the back tank. There's a hell of a lot of weight in all that water." He looked round all their faces. "Does anyone have an idea of how much water the fish needs to survive? I'm not an expert on catfish, but I've heard they can cope with poorish water quality."

Aghast looks told him the plan was not an option: they all thought too much of Gobblemouth to hazard his health at this stage.

In the end, they decided to stay put while Giles and Zofia sped ahead to the nearest town to see if he could find a garage with a breakdown truck and winch to heave the truck's tail-end back onto the road. Having Zofia with them was a blessing, Giles thought -

alone, it would not have been easy to explain the predicament to someone with no English.

***

"Come back to the campervan," Kendal invited the remaining crew. "I'll make us some tea while we wait. I've only got paralysed milk I'm afraid, but it won't be too bad."

All agreed except Derek Jones, who insisted on staying to guard the lorry.

"Nice to get away from the flies," said DeAvila as they all pushed their way into the tiny interior. Mike, last in, closed the door, but minutes later there was a frantic banging on the van's side. It was Derek Jones. He was now looking even more worried.

"Come quick," he yelled, "The tank - it's leaking."

Unnoticed while they had been building the now-unwanted ramp, water had been seeping out of the seal surrounding the covered drainage tap at the bottom of Gobblemouth's tank: it must have received a severe rap when the truck halted abruptly, shunting the big container forward against the next tank. The cover itself had not been designed to be completely watertight - just protection against the weather - and the adhesives used to fix it in place had cracked down one side. A small but steady trickle of water was running down onto the truck bed and dripping through the planks.

"It's not much yet but I'm worried it's getting worse," said Derek, and as if in agreement there was a hefty thump on the inside of the tank.

"Oh dear, somebody isn't happy," was Kendal's dry understatement in response to Gobblemouth's agitation. "What are we going to do?"

"Something pretty quick - it's all running into the ditch and that'll make it softer than ever under the wheel," said Derek. "I ought to

117

take the lid of the broken cover off, but it's hard to tell the damage to the tap."

"How much water can we afford to lose - if we get back on the road, that is? I mean, can we get as far as we're going to go and drop the fish in?"

"I don't think so. I suppose there's a chance if we find suitable water to top up the tank along the way, but there's always the worry the leak could get worse. If it gets desperate we'll just have to let him go in whatever water's nearest, be it river, pond or lake. No, this is something we have to get bloody well sorted here and now, I'm afraid."

Derek produced the locking cover key but he was reluctant to use it: opening it would break the seal around the lid, and if it was helping for the moment to stop the water running out too fast it was better not to disturb matters. His dilemma was obvious to them all. It was left to DeAvila to make an observation.

"Glue over the cracks - would that do it?"

Derek was shaking his head before he finished.

"Too much pressure from inside for that. And if we did use glue, assuming we can find some, the solvents could dissolve the stuff that's already there."

"Maybe there's another way to tackle it? From the inside, perhaps?"

"Inside the tank, you mean? It's possible..."

They could see his mind working.

"It depends on whether there's damage to the tap seating where it joins the wall of the tank or if it's just cracked on the outside bit." He made a screwing motion with one hand as if he was just shutting off a tap. "I'd guess it's the tap that's taken a knock - it's near the top of the cover - unseating the washer. If that's the case, then yes, we

118

ought to be able to shove something in the end of the connector. The pipe isn't that big. A cork, something like that ought to do it. But if it's the tank shell itself that's split, then we really are in trouble."

"A wine bottle cork, perhaps?" Kendal volunteered, fighting off an image that had formed in his mind of struggling underwater to find and bung-up a small opening. His near-drowning in a Scottish loch a few years back had left him with a dread of being submerged, let alone the possibility of being accompanied by a large and possibly angry catfish.

"Well, yes - but perhaps a bit bigger. I can't exactly recall the pipe diameter," said Derek. "Shall we take a look in - we might be able to measure it near-enough by eye."

***

Gobblemouth did not take at all kindly to having a bright flashlight shone down into his eyes while one person after another clambered onto the top of the tank to peer at him. He hated the extra light, sunlight especially. Back in the place he had come to know as 'home', Brightwell Lake, he would snooze through spring, summer and autumn days in one of a few chosen spots around the water where vegetation kept the rays dimmed, or deep, soft ooze where he could bury himself until the sun sank at the day's end. Then he could go on patrol, all his considerable senses on the alert, and find himself something to fill his large, hungry belly, until a newly rising sun told him it was time to nap again. His consignment first to a shallow pond, then for the last few days to a small, confining tank which was always on the move, was not helping his temper, and the one redeeming feature was that it was almost continually dim with the lid closed. Oh, and people kept chucking him food, which was nice but, given the chance, he'd rather catch his own. Now they were shining lights into his eyes, thumping the sides of his tank to jangle the line of pressure-sensitive nerves along his flanks, and apparently reducing the amount of water he had to move around in. Time to tell them he wasn't at all pleased about this, perhaps? Show how ferocious he could be? A display of aggression was the tactic that had shown off many a foe, from large pike to stalking spear-billed birds, even an otter that was all teeth, claws and fur.

However, all at once the activity ceased, and although he could still hear voices not far away his tank lid had been closed and everyone was down off the truck. The motivation for his grand protest faded away and he started switching off his muscle alerts and began to settle down. But this peace was not to last for long. Two people climbed up on the truck again and approached his tank, although this time they were moving with some caution, as if they did not want to alarm him. Nevertheless he again raised his level of alert.

***

"Are you ready?"

DeAvila gently opened the hatch on the tank and looked in: the dark shape of the big fish below looked quiet enough but there was no telling how it would behave once he dropped in beside it. The big landing net, minus its handle, which he intended to scoop the fish into to immobilise it, seemed a flimsy weapon against that bulk. But the situation was desperate and there did not seem to be any other way. Once he had the fish in the net, or as large a part of it as he could manage, he would try to hold its body against one side of the tank while Mike Cook joined him and found the end of the pipe connecting to the tap on the outside. In case of difficulties both men had ropes around them which Kendal and Derek Jones could haul on from the outside to get them out rapidly.

The group had been about to draw lots for what might prove to be a dangerous assignment, but DeAvila had quickly put himself forward as the best candidate, saying he felt somehow responsible for the situation after all he had put them all through. Mike had jumped at being the one to carry out the operation of blocking the pipe from the inside. Despite protests from Derek Jones and Mark Kendal he won the day, although Kendal was the most worried of all about letting his young companion be exposed to such a risky task. In spite of his heightened fear of water he would have done it, but he did have to admit that Mike was the fitter of them both. And wise words from Derek Jones sealed the arrangement: "They need us two on the outside as well - we're all part of the team."

Now that the moment was here, Mike's hands were shaking. Like DeAvila he was stripped down to a pair of shorts, and in one hand he held one of Kendal's stout cork pike fishing floats, pared down to a rough approximation of the size of the pipe's diameter. In the other was Kendal's large Bowie knife, still in its sheath, which he was to drop down into the tank ahead of his descent. Once he joined it and forced enough of the cork into the pipe to seal it, the plan was to saw the protruding end off flush so that Gobblemouth did not knock it and disturb the seal. For some of the operation Mike would have to have his head completely under the water.

"Ready?" Pedro DeAvila reached down as far as he could and let the net go so that it fell with hardly a splash and settled on the bottom beside Gobblemouth, who stirred uneasily. Mike let the Bowie knife follow it and was relieved when the object grounded not far from the pipe.

"Here goes." Grasping the edges of the hatchway with both hands, DeAvila swung his body into the void and cautiously lowered himself. "Wait until I give the OK," he cautioned, and Mike poised himself as the man let go of the sides and ducked entirely into the tank, disappearing head and all. Seconds later, a rapid thrashing alarmed Mike and the others. Muttered oaths followed, and then after more thrashing, the top of DeAvila's tousled head appeared in the hatchway, his eyes just looking over the edge.

"I've got him in the net and I can pin him against the side with my knees - but not for long, that's a strong fish," he said, chiefly for Mike's information. "Your turn now. Come on in - the water's lovely!"

The head disappeared and , screwing up his courage and gripping the makeshift bung in his mouth, Mike swung himself over the edge and into the tank. The experience of being engulfed by foetid air in semi-darkness was anything but lovely.

The water turned out to be much warmer than he'd imagined it would be. He felt for the bottom with his toes, while grunts of exertion from behind told him DeAvila was doing his best to restrict Gobblemouth's movements. A feeling of claustrophobia was almost overwhelming. But gradually his eyes were adjusting to the dim light. With his feet firmly on the bottom, the water was just below his armpits but he now needed to almost submerge himself to locate the pipe, searching with his fingertips. Derek Jones had asked him to be particularly careful when he got this far, taking the trouble to feel for any cracks which might reveal the damage was worse than they all hoped. "If you can also look as hard as you can as well it would help," he had said. "I know it will be dark and you can't see all that well underwater, but I hope you can try."

What Mike found close to the bottom of the tank was a piece of threaded pipe that protruded no more than a quarter of an inch, if that. A large flat octagonal nut and an even wider rubber washer, presumably tightened against a similar nut and washer on the other side, made a watertight seal with the side of the tank. The jutting piece of the pipe had been filed smooth so that it could not damage the tank's inhabitant if it brushed against it, and this would perhaps make it easier for Mike to push in the shaped cork float which was now floating loose on the surface of the water. He couldn't feel any new cracks or other damage when he ran his finger round the outside of the nut. Surfacing to take a deep breath, he upended himself to take a look. There was a lot of suspended matter this close to the bottom which he didn't want to think about, and he was aware of a renewed struggle going on behind him as he peered at the pipe: so far as he could make out from a few inches away all was well. Out of breath by this time he surfaced again to tell the others the good news. Behind, DeAvila was bracing himself against the tank walls and kneeling heavily against the fish. Reading his face, Mike saw he was having a hard time keeping the monster trapped, but the man forced a grin to his face and grunted: "Good luck - take your time and make a good job of it." Mike snatched up the bung and ducked back under to tackle his task.

Mark Kendal had worked hard at hacking down the big fishing float and smoothing it all off. It now looked like a stumpy cork carrot with a progressive taper. The narrow end fitted easily into the pipe, but because it was far wider at the broad end it became harder and harder to push it any further the deeper it went.

"Got most of it in," Mike bobbed up and reported to the outside.

"Give it an extra shove to make sure," came a muffled rejoinder from Kendal.

A sudden yelp from DeAvila made him look round.

"The brute's wriggling backwards and he very nearly nipped my foot," the man grimaced. "I'm not sure I can pin him down much longer. Are you nearly done?"

"Almost," Mike said to reassure him, ducking again to feel for the knife. It came to hand without much trouble but as he was about to pull it from its leather sheath there was another heavy flurry of activity from behind him.

"Sorry," said DeAvila. "He's getting more determined."

The next bit of the operation was critical, Mike told him, so an extra effort to quieten the big fish was needed. If Gobblemouth got away while he had a sharp open blade in his hand - or even if it dropped to the tank floor - there was no telling how much damage might be done. Trying not to think too hard about that, he pulled the knife out of its sheath, felt for the pipe again and started to saw at the cork.

***

Tension was just as high for the two watchers. Sundry bumps and thumps from inside did not help, especially when they could not see exactly what was going on. But the sound of a heavy engine approaching made them both look up. Minutes later, round the bend came Giles and Zofia in the Range Rover, and behind it was an enormous old-fashioned slab-fronted truck with a giant crane and hook on the back: the cavalry had arrived.

"What's going on?" Giles leaned out of his open window and asked as he drew up. Derek started to fill him in on the situation but he was interrupted by a sudden clatter as Mike's arm emerged from the tank and dropped the re-sheathed knife over the side. It was closely followed by his dripping head.

"Quick!" he yelled. "Help us out."

Derek and Kendal sprang into action and a dripping Mike was hauled out to stand shivering on the deck while they reached in to lift DeAvila, who cautioned: "You'll have to be quick - as soon as the pressure's off I've a feeling he could come after me. Grab my arms and I'll give you a count..."

They did as he asked, and on "three!" he popped out like a cork from a bottle. Behind, the water thrashed - the freed fish was determined to avenge his confinement, but clearly disappointed that the assailants had disappeared unscathed. DeAvila grinned - and his grin became even wider when he saw the crane.

Two very large and affable lads made short work of hitching the big hook under the tail of the truck to lift it and swing the rear wheels back onto the road. Arms covered up to the elbows in black engine oil, they'd clearly been interrupted during a routine maintenance job and were glad of the excuse to take a break. And after Zofia further explained the nature of their mission in Croatia, they steadfastly refused any payment for the rescue. One was particularly taken with their giant fish, which was still turning this way and that with irritation, and after climbing back down off the lorry he had an

124

animated conversation with Zofia which included a lot of arm stretching.

"He says there are much bigger ones in some of their rivers here," she interpreted. "He's caught some himself. But I don't think he understands why this one should be so important to us. I'm afraid he thinks you are all mad - but he expects that of the English!"

"He's probably right," said Giles, and as an afterthought: "I wonder if he's ever seen any crimson trout. Perhaps you could ask him?"

They saw both men shake their heads, but one of them reached into his overall pocket for an oily card which he passed to her before she thanked them once again and wished them farewell.

"No trout I guess?" said Giles as the truck headed off, its crane hook swinging like a cow swishing its tail to shoo off flies, and Zofia smiled.

"No. But they will ask around and tell us if they find out anything when - if - we come back this way. Or I can give them a call."

"How's the leak?" Giles asked. Derek climbed up to look at the outlet cover more closely.

"Doesn't seem any worse," he reported. "Time will tell, I guess. If we come across a suitable stream I'll stop and pump in some more water. I'll top up some of the other tanks too, to be on the safe side. And we'd better get that net out before the old boy gets strangled by it."

Gobblemouth refused the herring Kendal threw to him before the convoy set off again; he was still far too tetchy to think about eating - a rare state of mind for a catfish!

***

They made a stop for a quick coffee and snacks to restore everyone's spirits at the first suitable roadside halt. Mike found it had

125

a wireless connection and he took the opportunity to email news of their breakdown back to Vicky. He was sitting at a small table with Zofia as he click-clacked away on the keyboard. Suddenly she leaned across the table and said, eyes twinkling mischievously and disarmingly: "And how is your lover-girl? And the boss man with the broken leg?"

Mike felt himself blushing like a beetroot right to the roots of his hair.

"Sh-she's fine," he stammered, adding: "Actually, she keeps telling me to be more careful. But she's not my lover. She's not even my girlfriend."

"Oh," said Zofia, arching her eyebrows, "Then why does she act like it?"

With that she winked and let him off the hook by rising and going up to the bar to make yet another inquiry about crimson trout.

Mike's last email to Vicky was: "Please don't tell my mum about the tank. Mike, X."

Even without anyone watching, he was blushing again as he pressed 'Send'.

***

Their route now lay due east to a place called Osijek, a large and busy city hugging the banks of the River Drava, which itself might have made a final destination for Gobblemouth had it not already been decided that the plan was to take him to the Danube. But since the Drava had only a short distance to run after Osijek before it flowed into the Danube, their objective did not now seem to be all that far away.

Reaching the city was an opportunity to stretch their legs, eat and finalise plans. Mike and Kendal of course felt drawn to the river, running through the northern edge of the town. There were many fishermen on its banks and they stopped to watch one drawing in small silver fish, one after another. Moving off along the promenade and the colourful moorings below the Hotel Osijek, Kendal observed: "They've made the most of the waterside. It's beautiful. And it's a shame we haven't got time to fish."

Osijek was their parting place with Zofia. She had made friends with everyone since being 'sprung' as a stowaway, riding with everyone in turn, and had chattered informatively about the countryside as they made progress - even the fishing. She told Kendal all about her early days and catching bitterling, goldfish and baby carp and catfish for fairground prizes.

"Catfish, eh - did you ever send some to England?" he said jokingly.

"No, but I might have taken some there in person," she said, and told the tale of her trip for the family wedding, adding: "But I cannot remember if there were catfish. It is too long ago."

She fulfilled one more vital task: there were many fishing clubs in the area and she telephoned a handful to ask if anyone knew of special red trout. She gained no such information, alas, but the clubmen did promise to ask around and call Kendal or Mike if they heard of anything. But even without her usefulness as an interpreter, she would be missed.

Everyone got an energetic hug before she left, and even the still-sulking Gobblemouth was blown a kiss through the hatch of his tank. She was off on another mission: Giles drove her to the station where she caught a train to Budapest via Pecs.

"You lead an exciting life," he said. "Don't you ever tire of this sort of business?"

"It suits my nature," she replied with one of her flashing smiles. "I cannot stay in one place too long. It is in my blood."

***

She cut a far more romantic figure than Pedro DeAvila. Since the cash handover it would now have been hard to tell he was anything but a bona fide member of the fish delivery crew, and a companionable one at that now that he had dropped all the pretence. But before leaving Osijek they were reminded of his alter ego when a now fairly familiar Peugeot drew up and whisked him away for a private briefing. He came back with a serious look.

"I'm getting some laundry to take back to England," he said. "Don't know where, don't know when - but it will probably be in the next few days. I don't think the risk factor is very high, at least for anyone but me, unless there's something we haven't heard about. So far as the smuggling mob is concerned, I think I've delivered all the way along the line. But if anyone knows or suspects what I'm really doing they might have it in for me."

He shrugged.

"It goes with the territory. I just want you to know so that you won't be surprised if things go wrong for me. If there's a problem that puts you in danger I'll have to disappear on the pretext I thought the police were on to me and should make my own way home. By the way, if any of you get asked anything at all about me, your story is you don't know much about me - I am just an extra hand who was hired back in England to help with an ordinary task. Well, if carrying a catfish halfway across Europe can be considered an ordinary job, that is."

***

The country they plunged into beyond Osijek was little short of magical, especially for the fishermen of the party: they had left behind farming country and here there was forest and water in abundance, lakes, swamps and streams. Little wonder the Drava-Danube basin was known as 'Europe's Amazon' (Mike read from his guide book), and it contains reserves for rarities like the white-tailed eagle as well as hosting any number of fish species including the Danube salmon, one of the rarest fish in Europe and a species capable of growing to 100lb or more. Kendal was intrigued to hear about these big fish and wondered aloud what it took to catch one - a big spinner, perhaps, and certainly strong tackle.

"I bet you're sorry you left your pike gear at home," Mike said - both of them had light coarse fishing kit as well as fly rods for catching the crimson trout, should such a fish ever materialise. Kendal nodded. "I wouldn't mind. Come to think of it, I wouldn't mind taking a holiday around here some time."

"Me too," said Mike, but his attention was distracted by a large flock of big birds circling in a thermal up ahead. Closer, he could see that they were pelicans, soaring on enormous wings. Already he had spotted golden eagles and many storks, sights so un-English they would make a lasting impression.

They saw their final destination, Aljmas, before they reached the little town's outskirts - or rather, they saw a curiously-shaped high tower, huge.

"Nearly there," said Kendal. Just as well, because the light was going and it had been a doubly tiring day, all in all. Booked ahead for all the now much-travelled party were comfy rooms, and hopefully a good supper. Wearily, he guided the campervan with the Satnav's directions to the town centre.

Mike was still intrigued by the tower. As they got nearer, its shape growing even more curious. Finally they drove into a square which surrounded the huge modernistic structure, which finally revealed itself as a church. It was not this which now made Mike's jaw drop, however, but two figures he saw standing outside it. One, leaning on a crutch, was Michael Tipton. The other was Vicky Price!

***

Far too embarrassed other than to mumble 'Hello' to Vicky, Mike stepped forward and took the handshake offered by the Earl of Sparhill.

"Ah, young Mike - surprised to see us, eh?" he said while Vicky looked on, her eyes laughing. "We flew in to Osijek yesterday and decided to come on ahead rather than hunt you down through the town."

Kendal, who had just parked the van, came to join them, receiving another warm handshake.

"Hello sir," said Kendal, which made Tipton shake his head.

"No 'sirs'," he said, "Michael or Mike will do. I grew out of my airs and graces long ago. The doctors have let me off the hook so long as I travel with suitable care, and I think Vicky here is very suitable. Come along, we'll escort you to your B&B. We're all meeting there for supper shortly. Bet you're ready for a bite to eat, eh? Your companions have told me you've all had an adventurous time. Wish I could have been there! "

Mike Cook fell in step with Vicky behind Tipton and Kendal. He felt awkward and unable to think of anything to say at first, but she broke the ice. Gently, she took his arm.

"So I missed all the excitement. Just my luck."

"It was a bit scary...well, quite a bit scary, actually."

"What, messing with the smugglers or climbing into a tank with a giant fish?"

"Both."

She laughed. "Well, it wasn't all that bad following your exploits from afar," she said. "And don't worry, I didn't scare your mum. But I have seen her and so far as she knows everything has been running smoothly."

"Thanks for that," he said gratefully.

***

The meal was a high-spirited affair, with the host family joining in the fun that followed - they had invited local musicians to join the

130

party after eating. But before that, everyone had talked about the conclusion - or one of the two conclusions - of their trip on the next day.

It had still not been resolved how they were to transfer Gobblemouth, who had entered the tank through its only hatch on the top, into the river - a river none of them except Tipton and Vicky had yet seen.

"Don't worry," Tipton said to conclude the discussion. "I've made some arrangements and it's all taken care of. And you'll all be ready for it after a good night's rest." Just what the arrangements were, Tipton would not say and he refused to be drawn on the matter.

As well as local folk songs and tunes, the musicians - a fiddler, a guitar player and an excellent accordion-player - rendered some well-known Country and Western tunes, with everyone joining in as best they were able. In between, they heard the story of the village, which had seen many inhabitants driven out during the Balkan wars, with their homes and possessions taken over by others and their beloved old Marian church burnt to the ground by the Yugoslav army. Rebuilt in 2006, the modernist building was still a bone of contention among the locals, the architecture loved or loathed in equal measure.

In one of the energetic and bewildering partner-changing folk dances Mike found himself with Vicky as the music ended. Still holding her hand as they left the floor, he was about to sit down when she tugged him, leaned closer and whispered: "Come along. Wouldn't you like to take a look at the river?"

***

It was pleasantly cool outside but Mike was aware of little but the pressure of the hand he still held, and for a while they said nothing, just walked. The gradually sloping streets led them away from the centre, where all was very quiet except for the odd figure on some errand and a few cats. And then, turning one last corner, they were

131

on a road parallel to a broad, dark waterway, with houses and gardens to their right.

"Wow. Is that the Danube?"

Even in the dark Mike could see the river was it was impressively big, and to its far side forest ran down to the water's edge. A few street lights gave extra gloss to the dark and fast moving water. The river smells, lingering with the scent of late roses in some of the gardens, were almost tangible.

"It certainly is. We came down here this morning - we're only a few miles down from the confluence with the Drava, a major tributary," Vicky said informatively. "The river is a big thing with the locals, as you can appreciate. And they're all as fishy as you and your pals - no wonder we're all getting on so well."

Then, all of a sudden, she tugged his hand, stopping. Her face came closer.

"Mike Cook - tell me you have another girlfriend and I'll let you go right now."

He was blushing again, he knew it, but this time it was because he was aware her voice was affecting him on many different levels at once. But something was wrong with his own powers of speech, and he couldn't articulate an answer, no matter how hard he tried.

"I..I.."

"Shh," she said, and her lips brushed first his cheek and then, ever so softly, his lips. And the words no longer mattered.

***

Mike wasn't certain how long they stood there before the voices of a passing elderly couple made him - both of them, really - aware they were on public display.

"Come along," he said. "The others will be wondering what has happened to us."

132

"Do you really think so?" she said with a mischievous laugh. "You're not so smart as you like people to think."

Chapter 11

If Gobblemouth was not exactly aware of where in the world he was, at least he knew the sounds of waterbirds when he heard them - and now the noises were so close they made him yearn for freedom, open water. After days in close confinement, his plastic prison was getting to him in a big way. The only good thing was that he had stopped moving. It was morning, he'd heard the approach of a big vehicle and people were again looking down at him from above.

He nosed disinterestedly at the herring that had been thrown to him, even picked it up and rolled it between his big rough bony lips, but he could not bring himself to swallow it and instead spat it out, sending it twirling away in a vortex of expelled water.

"Not a happy bunny," observed an echoing voice from the sky - Derek Jones knew his fish, even if he had never had much to do with giant Danube catfish. "I'd say he couldn't put up with this much longer."

Although he was by now used to having his water level adjusted, Gobblemouth was surprised when a stout hose was lowered in and quite a large amount was drawn away. And even more surprisingly, another hose was lowered in and fresh water poured all around him - fresh, cool water full of exciting tastes and smells.

"A bit of river water. That'll help him adjust a bit to where he's going, I hope," said the voice, muffled now Derek's head was outside the tank. There were other voices too, quite a lot of voices, but the big fish ignored these and nosed around until he found the herring, his appetite miraculously aroused by the sense that something was afoot.

***

The scene in the square was busy not only with people going about their daily business but also with an excited knot of spectators who had gathered with curiosity around the big fish-transporter. Beside it too were members of the local fire brigade with their fire engine, and an enormous yellow-and-green Russian tractor rigged with a rear hoist and winch.

Mike, suffering more than a little from another thick head, found Michael Tipton busily directing things. Giles, Pedro DeAvila and Derek Jones were there too, but a notable exception was Vicky. He was disappointed but he tried to make himself appear as cheerful as possible.

"Good morning, Sir. Anything I can do to help?"

The offer was politely refused, but the Earl added with a smile: "Come along anyway - I expect you're keen to see an end to your mission. It's not going to be as easy as we thought - there's a lot of extra water in the river this morning."

Derek climbed into the transporter driving seat and started the engine up. With a thumbs-up signal from Tipton, a little convoy started away from the square and headed in the direction of the river - ahead was the big tractor, followed by the transporter, with the fire engine with all its fire crew clinging to its sides behind that. Everyone else walked but that was all right, because the vehicles were not rushing off.

Mike recognised the route as the road he had taken with Vicky the night before - at the start it didn't look all that different in daylight (although a million times less romantic) but when they turned the corner which brought it alongside the river, the reason for the Earl's anxieties became clear. In just a few yards water was lapping on the surface and the gentle slope took the rest of it underneath the muddy swirl. The tractor, however, ploughed on until the water was up to its belly, while Derek executed quite a lengthy procedure to turn the lorry around so that its rear end - and Gobblemouth's tank - came to rest hanging over the water.

135

"There's been a lot of rain upstream on both rivers and the level came up suddenly overnight," Tipton explained. "These are huge rivers, longer than anything we've got, and it can be balmy summer at one end and raging tempest at the other. Rises like this used to take people by surprise but these days they know when it's coming. The Drava in particular has flooded miles and miles of land. Our side is really muddy because of this but the Danube's a bit clearer. The two lots of water haven't had chance to mix yet so the Danube downstream is brown on one side and clear on the other, for several miles it seems. Look, the gardens of those houses are right under water, never mind the road. A bit more water and the houseowners will get worried too."

Mike took it all in. The spot where he and Vicky had embraced had vanished under a swirl of muddy brown water, but he did not feel like telling anyone how romantic it had all looked around midnight, still less the outcome of his excursion.

The firemen swarmed onto the lorry and with DeAvila's direction started to thread heavy-duty canvas slings under Gobblemouth's chocked-up tank. Giles came over to Tipton.

"All set?" he said.

"Everything's ready."

Mike, curious, wanted to know what the procedure was to get the catfish out of his tank when the only entrance and exit was at the top.

"Ah," said the Earl, "I was wondering when somebody would ask me that. Well, I've had some time to think about it while you lot have been enjoying yourselves and this is how it goes. In a minute, when the hoist's hooked up, Pedro is going to remove the lid - look, he's unscrewing the hinge now. Then our friendly local tractor driver is going to lift the whole caboodle and chug down the road until he can lower it into deep water - the hoist has an extending hydraulic arm that can reach out several metres to the rear of the tractor. The fish will then be in a sort of floating goldfish bowl so to stop it

136

sailing away completely, fish and all, our friends the firemen are going to pump it full of water until it sits on the bottom."

"What then?" asked Mike. "He still isn't likely to jump out of the top."

"I was coming to that. Some brave soul is going to swim out to the tank and reset the slings around the bottom of the tank so that it won't shift any further back. Then the hoist arm will gently nudge the top of the tank back until it falls on its side - and the fish swims out, bingo! At least, that's the theory."

The earl sounded confident about this plan but the old scar across his face had turned white and Mike noticed his fists were tightly clenched, spelling inner tension. He was about to ask what they would do if any part of this plan went wrong but stopped himself. Apart from upsetting anyone, he did not want to be accused of manufacturing self-fulfilling prophesies. Fortunately, at this moment a swimmer in back wetsuit and flippers appeared at the water's edge like a picture that Tipton had conjured up to illustrate his plan. Pedro DeAvila sent the tank's plastic lid skidding noisily back towards them across the wet road, while the tractor winch hook gradually took up the strain on the hoist's webbing sling. What the earl called "Operation Gobblemouth" had started.

***

Swinging the tank slowly and steadily round in a wide arc the hydraulic arm steadied and then started to extend it to where the frogman was treading water. So far so good, thought Mike as the winch cable was unfurled until the tank's bottom touched the water and then carried on slowly sinking.

At this point the fire tender was driven as far into the water as it could go without compromising the engine and crew cab. A firefighter balancing at the far end of the extending turntable ladder was now also pushed forward above the tank so that the hose he carried could stream additional water in through the open top.

137

Then Mike's heart sank - things were suddenly starting to go wrong. The jet of water aimed for the tank opening missed its mark and gave the rig a violent twist. A moment later the tank was bobbing free of its webbing cradle.

But for the quick-wittedness of the Croatian tractor driver tank, fish and all might have sailed off there and then down to the Danube where it would be whisked away by the swollen and turbulent river. However, the man managed to squeeze another foot of reach out of the extending hydraulic arm and drop the hoist hook straight into the tank mouth. This was fishing on a grand scale!

Shouts of alarm silenced abruptly: everyone waited with bated breath to see what would happen next.

Inch by inch the tank moved towards the river while the winch cable tightened. The frogman wisely moved aside out of the way of the big swivel which briefly snagged the edge of the hatchway but them jerked free. Everything now depended on whether or not the hook itself was the right way round to get a grip on the lip of the opening.

The shank of the big lump of metal appeared and with another jolt the tank leaned towards the anxious watches and came to a halt. The desperate effort had worked, but the tank was far from safe even so.

"What now?" somebody shouted, but it was clear to all that the situation would not remain stable if the tank mouth continued to topple towards the watchers while its bottom lifted and pulled the other way. A gathering crowd murmured apprehensively.

However, yet more heroes appeared. The firefighters turned into the saviours of the day, along with the tractor driver. Heedless of their own safety and unconcerned how wet they got they produced two stout ropes as if by magic, ploughing out fully-clothed to insert poles into the tank's mouth so they they would jam cross the opening and anchor it more securely. The ropes were fastened on to these and the end of one was secured round a large tree while the other was tied to a stanchion on the fire tender. The firefighter still on the extended ladder dropped the end of his hose to his bobbing colleagues who inserted it in the tank's mouth and resumed pumping in water to sink it. Meanwhile the frogman churned off in search of the canvas sling which had been making its way steadily downstream. Catching it up he returned with it to his colleagues, who were now so soaked they no longer cared about being up to their necks in water. The webbing loops were fixed securely round the tank and once again hooked up to the tractor, which was backed gently until it took up the strain on the hoist cable.

Calm returned. Now that the drama was over the crowd started to drift away, encouraged to do so by approaching black clouds and the first large raindrops of an approaching storm. In no time at all the tank lay on its side on the bottom where planned, and in theory at least Gobblemouth could at last swim out and away, free in his native river. However, with the muddiness of the floodwater it would be impossible to witness when and if he took advantage of this opportunity ...

***

It had been a trying time for the big fish. Already out of sorts after being trucked across most of Europe in severely limited space, he'd had to put up with the thud of nearby large engines, shouting human beings and a lot of thumps and bumps on the outside of the tank. After that had come the unsettling experience of being hoisted, swaying in the air, before descending once again into the sounds of a renewed furore. What was going on?

Then there was a giddying lurch, and the additional sound of water slopping around the tank walls. The shouts had intensified at this point, and there was frenzied human activity in very direction before his whole world started toppling to one side...

More water poured in, and he tasted the river in it and the elusive scents and tastes of live fish. How odd that at the moment he sensed the most peril he at the same time received these signals of normalcy, and above all hope.

Confusingly, the direction he had long come to rely on as being 'up' and where people had occasionally thrown him food, was now becoming 'side', as was the secure area that he had once regarded as the bottom of this tiny world. His unconscious sense of balance helped him to adjust to all this. Then all fell quiet, at least in terms of human activity, and he now had a chance to try to make sense of his new situation.

***

"Well just leave him for a bit, see what happens," said Tipton, "unless you all want to stay here while this storm breaks."

Even the firemen, who could hardly have got much wetter, did not want to hang around: sweeping down from the North West where it had already swollen the Danube and the Drava, this was undoubtedly one of those first-of-the-year testing reminders that winter was not very far away. Besides, if there was further flooding or lightning damage - already rumbles of thunder could be heard - their services might be needed for real people-emergencies. After unhitching the temporary securing lines, closing the telescopic ladder and rolling up the hose, they were soon away, off up the road with a cheery wave to change clothes and get ready for what could well be a busy night ahead.

After making sure the last tether to the tank was holding and double-checking his brakes, the tractor driver switched off his big machine and joined Tipton, Giles and Mike making their way on foot back to the guest house where they had eaten the night before. Derek Jones and Pedro DeAvila went on ahead in the now empty and one-tank-lighter transporter which, for the moment at least, had completed its primary mission.

Although he would dearly like to see the instant Gobblemouth regained his freedom, it wasn't without anticipation that Mike Cook retraced his steps to the guesthouse - and Vicky. And the fact his head had at last cleared made his steps all the lighter.

***

The approaching storm held no fear for Gobblemouth. Indeed, it brought all his senses alive: even for a fish that had spent the best part of its life in still water, storms meant food, if not from the silt they stirred up or washed from the bank then certainly from the confusion of inexperienced small fish and other creatures, and their vulnerability in poor light.

Gobblemouth loved poor light: he'd been beautifully designed to take advantage of all that it offered, and it was in a state of full alert that something amazing happened - a gudgeon swam into the tank and set all that super-tuning jangling. It was the first live fish he had seen in some considerable time and it was astonishing, magical.

But after only a few seconds the newcomer turned tail and fled, no doubt itself sensing a menacing presence. However the sighting encouraged Gobblemouth draw cautiously closer to the hole in the tank through which the little fish had come.

With his wide-set eyes he could not see far ahead through the opening, but the information that was flooding in as tastes and smells was more than intriguing: there were clearly other fish out there, many of them identifiable by characteristic scents: roach, bream, carp. There were sounds too - the minute clicks and squeaks of nearby small fish, the calls of water birds. Slowly, he edged his great head out, and although he feared nothing after a life in an environment where nothing had ever challenged him, he was naturally cautious in an unfamiliar setting. Further out still, he could see and sense more - and up, down, to each side as far as he could make out, there was unrestricted water.

A flash of lightning penetrated the water and the thunder came almost instantly, meaning the towering storm cloud was right overhead. Emboldened by the lack of a perceived threat,

Gobblemouth flexed the cramped and over-idle muscles of his long body to slide entirely out of his prison, turning on his tail suddenly to confront it in case it would attack and engulf him again. For the first time he realised it was completely inanimate, a cave of plastic with no more menace than a sunken tree trunk. Just to make sure of this he circled it slowly three times, wider and wider, realising as he did so that it lay on a slope leading down into deeper and deeper water.

It was from this water that the fish signals were coming and he suddenly realised he was very, very hungry for real prey. Needing no more motivation than that he moved himself steadily forward, deeper and deeper, almost certainly the only catfish that had come all the way from England to swim free into the great River Danube down one of Aljmas's streets.

***

"He's gone! He's gone!"

They all looked round. Mike had been down to the tank to find the floodwater had receded enough for him to peer through the opening: the silt had settled and the water was relatively clear. A couple of luckless small gudgeon that would soon find themselves trapped if they didn't get out were hugging the bottom, but the big fish that the group had cosseted for days on end had gone.

It was a triumph for the project, but at the same time anti-climax showed on all the faces gathered around the cafe table where they had been trying to explain the concept of afternoon tea to the natives.

Tipton was the first to speak, seeking to emphasise the positive.

"Brilliant! Well done everyone."

He raised his mug of tea and clashed it with his brother's. "Here's to good luck for Gobblemouth!"

Derek Jones looked the most relieved: he'd become increasingly worried about the health of the last fish in his charge for the outward journey, and now that Gobblemouth had conveniently let himself out of his jail it was a big weight off his shoulders.

"Cheers. I'll go and get the tank mounted up again right away, and we can leave in an hour or so, maybe - we're almost back on schedule."

When he had gone, Mike wondered out aloud how Gobblemouth might get on in his new and very unfamiliar surroundings. Kendal had been pondering much the same thing and told the group he thought the fish might be a good distance downriver by now because of his unfamiliarity of dealing with a current of any kind - let alone a flooded river which still had some pace even if the levels were falling.

"But I have no doubt he'll cope with that quite quickly, or at least find a slack area where it isn't so much of a problem," he said. "But it's my bet the first thing on his mind will be food, and there will be plenty of that around. And long term he's got no real worries about being attacked by other fish - even though there are monsters in this river, especially of his own kind, he's simply too big to be eaten. And it isn't the breeding season so he won't be challenged on that score. Interestingly, once he's found a partner he'll be the one in charge of looking after the eggs and protecting the hatchlings until they can fend for themselves."

"So it's really all over," said Mike, not without a pang of disappointment.

"Yes and no," said Tipton. "We still don't have any crimson trout for Roger Percy, do we?"

***

They'd tried hard enough to find these elusive trout, their Holy Grail, but it had been fruitless: not a word from any of the people they had contacted along the way and who they'd asked to message them if anything came to light. Roger Percy's attempts from England to contact anyone who might be able to help had similarly drawn a blank.

Now, albeit they had the background of the successful delivery of Gobblemouth to the Danube, the reality of going home empty-handed loomed large.

With the tank re-loaded, the plan was to head back for Osijek where they could reassemble briefly before Derek Jones and Pedro DeAvila took the truck back through Italy, then France, with bits of business to pick up on the way. Tipton had managed to book a flight home late that evening for himself and Vicky, while Giles would take them both to the airport then take fast roads home more or less non-stop in the Range Rover.

"I can probably get you on a flight tomorrow morning," Tipton offered Mike when they were all packed, "Or you can go with Giles." But Kendal had another idea.

"If you like, Mike, you can stick with me. The van's a bit slower, as you know, and I plan to do a bit of fishing on the way back."

Mike was due back at work in a few days, otherwise he'd have jumped at the chance. There was also his mother to consider - she would worry, he knew, even though he regarded himself as grown up.

"Perhaps I can help?" Vicky was smiling and he realised parting once again from her was going to be quite hard.

"Don't worry - I'll tell your mum and I can assure her you'll be well looked after. And as for work, perhaps you can write a note or something for me to deliver, or better still send me an email I can bounce on to them. Tell them to knock the extra days off your holiday allowance, something like that? After all you've been through you could do with some R and R. The paper won't stop publishing because you're not there. You will look after him, won't you Mr Kendal?"

Kendal grinned. "Like a baby," he said. Kendal also waved away Mike's offer to pay his way for himself. "It'll hardly cost any more than for one," he said. And so that was that. Despite a reassuring hand squeeze from Vicky, the thought crossed Mike's mind that he'd just let himself in for another spell of Kendal's diabolical snoring.

***

It was a darkening road through the woods back towards Osijek that evening. Kendal was unusually quiet, which didn't help a descending mood of gloom. Mike was the first to break a long silence.

"He will be all right, won't he?"

"The fish, you mean?"

"Yes. That's what you're thinking about, isn't it?"

"Ay, I was ... and yes, on balance I'd say he was OK. They're pretty tough, catfish. But I'm wondering now it's all over it might have been a bit of a silly adventure. We've come a long. long, long way just for this, when we could have put him back where he came from. Or somewhere else just as amenable as Brightwell ... somewhere closer that's for sure."

"But it has been a bit of a lark, hasn't it? A lot of fun, at least in retrospect."

That made Kendal laugh.

"Well yes, we've got a lot out of it. And another thing is he's now got a chance to meet others of his kind and, well, fulfil himself, you know."

The mood lifted somewhat, but another silence fell. When Mike spoke again it was on a different topic but one that had worried him for some time. Kendal might just be the person to talk to about it.

"Did you enjoy being a journalist, before you retired, I mean?"

Kendal thought for a moment.

145

"Do I think it's a good career choice?"

"Something like that. Only we - the paper I mean - we seem to be going downhill, at least as far as sales go. I know the editor's worried about it."

"I'm sure that's right - all papers, not just yours. But you have online editions, surely? That's the future, so far as I see it. We can't alter progress, we can only adapt to it - incidentally, do you know Darwin never said 'survival of the fittest' was the key to evolution. Instead, it was survival of the most adaptable, and there's a lesson in that for everyone. I saw plenty of changes in my time. In the fifties and sixties, for example, do you know the factor that sold the most newspapers? You won't guess it, so I'll tell you - it was the racing results sent by wire and printed in a 'stop-press' panel on the back page, because the man in the street didn't have the means of getting that information quickly at the time. Most betting was highly illegal and bets were placed with runners who took bets to the bookmakers. So just a few lines of hard information was selling thousands of papers at that point - but when radio and television, came alone, and bookies shops with their own results service, the stop-press meant nothing. The papers that survived realised that they had to become very much more entertaining than merely supplying information. On top of that local journalism has always been particularly valuable for the community - when I was your age the paper I worked for exposed a particularly nasty piece of local government corruption, and the reporter who broke it said to me, 'That's what we're here for laddie - to keep the bastards honest'. To my mind that was a good reason for adapting and keeping the tradition going - even if I still prefer reading my printed newspaper. And as for the editor being worried...well, as time goes by you'll realise that editors are always worried about something."

Lots of material to chew on. Mike couldn't think immediately of anything to say, and after a minute Kendal said anxiously: "I hope that helps. Does it?"

"Yes. And I must send them my latest report when I think of it. Pity we never got the crimson trout, though - have we done enough to try and find them, I wonder?"

Kendal shrugged. "Well, we can hardly go up into the mountains and fish every lake we find, can we ... enticing though the notion is. No, we've asked everyone we can and nothing has come up. Look..."

He nodded ahead to the approaching town lights.

"We're nearly in Osijek again. Time to say our goodbyes and get on our way."

***

The next day, an exciting spell fishing on the River Drava 'for whatever comes along' in Kendal's words lifted Mike's spirits a little, but in truth a part of him was wishing he'd taken up the offer of a flight home.

But that was before the crimson trout came along - three of them, that is, for each of them, fragrantly grilled and presented for their dinner by a beaming restaurant owner back at the mountain park where they had delivered the last of the rainbows not so long ago.

Chapter 12

They were clearly truly remarkable fish, even when cooked to a turn!

"You see - we find them for you!"

The little fish had glowing scarlet skins flecked with lighter orange spots and there was a deeper shade of red in a line along their backs, nose to tail. The throat area had an even more distinctive area of bright crimson, like an American cut-throat trout. Inside the flesh was if anything more striking still, as red as very rare beef.

"Well done - really well done!" Kendal responded to the delighted restaurateur's excitement with a beam of his own and matching enthusiasm.

Mike was simply dumbstruck; secretly, he had started to doubt if the fish ever truly existed. They tasted as good as they looked.

Between mouthfuls, Kendal enquired where their surprise meal had come from, and learned they were in a mountain lake which, although not very far away, was difficult to access and therefore rarely visited. Before he left their table, the man said he would arrange for a guide to take them there but wondered how they might bring them back alive since it was a long way from a road or even a track that could be used by a motor vehicle.

"We'll have to leave that for the future," he said. "I don't suppose you have any more of them, in your freezer perhaps?"

The man shook his head.

"In that case, we'll go tomorrow, if that's all right. All I need is a couple of specimens to freeze and we'll do our best to get them to an airport to send back to Roger Percy, unless somebody can think of a better plan."

Mike was shaking his head when a sudden afterthought struck him - why not email Vicky and see what Percy thought about the discovery? Remembering that the fish merchant had his own small aircraft capable of carrying live elvers, he wondered if some alternative plan could not be worked around this fact.

"I agree," said Kendal. "But let's finish our dinner first. The fish are delicious, but let's hope they're not the last of their kind, eh? That would be a tragedy."

And a bit later another comment, out of the blue: "What if we hadn't called back here?"

The last of the diners had left and the tables were being tidied for the morning when Mike got a message back from Vicky.

"The boss says to hold on there if you can. He's going to find a nearby airstrip and I'm going to have a sleepless night organising permissions to fly halfway across the world, let alone dealing with import and export regs. I'd love to join him but I'm afraid the fish come first for him and he needs all the space he can get. I am so looking forward to seeing you again - in one piece if at all possible. Love, Vicky XXX"

"Does waiting for Percy mean we can't go fishing tomorrow? I was hoping we could at least make a recce," Kendal said.

Mike wasn't thinking about fish at that moment but he brought himself back to the matter in hand.

"We can leave directions. We'd only be kicking around doing nothing otherwise. We could be doing something useful, like setting up a base camp - and we'll have to learn how to catch some of the fish. No way of knowing how easy or difficult that might be."

"Good."

At last Mike felt his spirits lifting and realised that something had been missing from his life in the last couple of days since they left the side of the Danube. It was adventure.

***

"Why is he carrying a gun?"

They had the restaurant owner's 20-year old son Spiros along as an interpreter, but this was a question he did not have to translate for their guide, a big-bearded, burly man dressed - and armed - as if he was going on a commando raid. Spiros had brought his own rod, a short and ancient split-cane affair with two lengths held together with elastic bands.

"The gun? Oh, that'll be for the bears," said the young man off-handedly. "I don't think we'll have any trouble but you can't be too sure."

"Bears?" Mike was incredulous. He hadn't realised this was bear country. The tingle of danger gave added spice to the expedition as well as reminding him there were parts of the world a good deal wilder than anything he'd yet encountered in his life.

"I guess our fishing rods wouldn't be a great deal of use against them," said Kendal drily.

"You could snore," said Mike, wickedly. "They wouldn't hang around for very long."

"Come," said the guide, grinning and pointing to the steeply inclined track leading away from the roadside parking spot and disappearing into a heavy mist. He set off and they followed with their light packs and fly rods, trying to keep up with his long strides. The lad was immediately behind him, with Kendal and Mike trailing.

Kendal turned his head after a little while and said: "Are you all right back there? We could take it in turns if you like. But I don't think the bears are going to get you."

"Fine."

"You know, in Canada people sew little bells into their jackets to frighten off the bears when they go into the wilderness. It works most of the time. But..."

"But?" said Mike, the hanging sentence giving him a twinge of anxiety.

"But then they say there are two kinds of bears and only one of them wants to eat you. You can tell the one from the other if you find any bear poo. One kind is sweet-smelling and full of seeds and bits of grass and vegetation, and that sort is OK because that's a vegetarian bear which will be driven off by the bells and won't be interested in attacking you. But the other kind of poo is dark and smelly rather like the one we've just passed - and full of little bells, so then you know you're in real trouble."

He turned and grinned.

"That gets you back for the snoring remark."

Shortly after that, they stepped quite abruptly into clear air and bright sunlight, and a few paces further on and they could see a blanket of mist spread below them with just a few distant peaks showing through. Ahead, the figure leading them with a gun slung over his shoulder turned and waved them on and plodded forward again.

"He says it is not far now," their interpreter informed them.

***

When they finally reached the lake after the strenuous climb through myrtle and juniper scrub they found it was not a very big water - nine or ten acres at the most, with a shoreline of broken black rocks. Closer, they made out a series of small bays lined with dark sand. For the moment at least, the calm surface looked quite lifeless. The water itself was very clear, and they could see the bottom for some distance out.

"Not ever so promising," said Kendal, throwing his rucksack down and starting to unpack his rod. "Still, if this really is the place we'd batter get started. I haven't done a lot of fly fishing, but I'd say we were looking at very small dark flies, gnats maybe, fished dry on light leaders - light as you can go. It's very like some of the Scottish hill lochs I've fished. Get set up and I'll choose you something to have a go with."

His work completed, their guide found himself a sandy spot where he could stretch out facing the sun with his head on his pack. He promptly fell asleep. Spiros eagerly put up his own tackle, crude in comparison to the light carbon fibre fly rods and fine lines employed by Mike and Kendal. After threading his stout and curly nylon line through the rusting wire rod rings, he attached a large sliding drilled bullet and tied on an eyed size 10 hook. From the plastic carrier bag that held his tackle and lunch he produced a jar of brandling worms and impaled one before hurling it towards the centre of the lake. It whirred out trailing a long arc of line and landed with a resounding 'plop!'. After tightening the line he propped the rod against a rock and then he himself lay down with his hands behind his head.

"Good luck," he said, squinting at them in the sunlight before closing his eyes. Mike caught a glance from Kendal who was rolling his eyes.

"Well, I guess it's a tried and tested method round these parts," he said. "Let's go, shall we."

They made their way steadily from bay to bay, initially without luck. After an hour of this, however, a slight breeze blew up and ruffled the calm surface, which was suddenly dimpled by rising fish.

"Any minute now," Kendal said to Mike, and even as he spoke his line tightened and he started playing a spirited little fish which, even at a distance, showed its striking colours whenever it skipped out of the water. Out of the corner of his eye Mike saw the nose of a fish head-and-tailing near his own fly, and a second or two later he tightened into a trout himself.

152

They weren't big - about six ounces apiece - but their capture marked the final objective of the adventure. Almost.

"I don't think we need any more than a couple of samples, do we?" said Kendal. "We'll put these two back and fish on - plenty of time to get more."

But despite hard fishing for another couple of hours, the helpful little breeze died away and there were no more catches for the pair. Disheartened, they approached Spiros and the genial guide with long faces having completed a full circuit of the mountain lake.

"No fish?" said Spiros brightly. "Never mind, come here."

He led them over to a boulder where, out of the heat of the sun, lay six beautiful little crimson trout.

"See - I have plenty for us," the young man said triumphantly.

***

Back at the guest house, Mike got a Skype connection though to Vicky. He had a lot to say, but looking at her face struck him dumb. He realised he was blushing again. Grinning, she said "Wait" and moved aside to let Roger Percy take her place in front of the computer camera.

"I hear you've had some luck," he said.

Coming back to his senses, Mike held up two of the trout in front of the camera.

"Well done!" said Percy. "Listen, there's no reason for you two to hang around there now - I've got clearance to come over the day after tomorrow and Vicky here has cleverly arranged with their fisheries people to let us electro-fish a corner of the lake and take some away - I'll fly them back myself. In fact, they're even supplying the fishing team - seems they're glad of me breeding some off site so that there's a restocking supply if anything every happens to the lake population. So if you want to move on, that's all right with me. But by all means stay if you want."

Looking over Mike's shoulder Kendal gave him a nudge. "Tell he we're up for staying - I wouldn't miss it for the world," he said.

"I heard that loud and clear," said Percy. "Look forward to that. But I've got a bit of bad news too, at least it may be bad news - hard to tell. But Pedro DeAvila's gone missing. It worried Derek Jones no end, but I was able to get some help for him via Toulouse airport so he's able to complete all the pick-ups. What's really happened to DeAvila we can't tell, but my man from the ministry has been round and he says he can look after himself and we shouldn't worry, but you do all the same, don't you? Anyhow, one good thing comes out of it - seems my fish transporter is no longer 'safe' transport for the bad boys. I'm glad of that - I'm a fishmonger, not a bloody branch of the Secret Service!"

***

To tie up some loose ends: Perhaps needless to say, the rest of the Quest for the Crimson Trout was concluded satisfactorily and quickly. The local game and wildlife people knew their stuff and Mike and Kendal had little to do but watch the netting operation, or risk getting in the way. Soon around 40 of the colourful little fish were winging their way, alive, back to England aboard Roger Percy's light plane. And he flew off with the promise that a watch would be kept on the lake's feeder streams for signs of spawning fish, with the dual purpose of collecting some fertilised ova and to fill in some missing gaps in what was known of the trout variety's biology and habits.

Trout are funny and adaptable little beasts: because in the distant past they survived a range of climatic conditions, including ice ages, in separation from one another in any number of deep lakes, they have since evolved and developed different characteristics to make themselves successful in their own environments. In many areas where they are widespread - Scotland, for example, as well as in the

154

Balkans - the trout of one lake look completely different to trout from another water - colour, perhaps, or a larger or lesser number of spots (including no spots at all).

One could also say people are similarly adaptable, and perhaps just as peculiar. In an age when the foodstuffs and cuisines from around the world have become familiar to most folk, the urge to try something different from the items on this menu (albeit a very large menu) is strong. This was the rationale behind Percy's plan to put crimson trout on plates - different, of course, but also extremely attractive. First, however, he wanted to try to create a sustainable supply. Whether or not this part of the quest was successful you will only find out when they turn up on a menu in a restaurant near you.

Mike Cook and Mark Kendal enjoyed their leisurely return to England. It's fair to say the young man who set out from home shores not a very long time ago was an older and wiser man. In terms of fishing alone he learned much from his older companion, but ahead lay a romance which was a subject about which Kendal steadfastly declined to give him any advice other than one recommendation. It was perhaps the same principal that had perhaps guided all the questers in their adventure: Pitch in and try it, or you will never know where it might take you.

Despite his unfortunate accident the trip did nothing to harm Michael Tipton, only reinforced his feeling that Brightwell was the nicest place on earth and he would do everything in his powers to protect it.

None of the principal players heard anything more at all about Pedro DeAvila. But then, maybe it isn't his real name after all.

PART TWO

1. The Storyteller

Bryn and Carol Thomas knew the letter had to be opened. Bryn's face had fallen when it came through the door at breakfast-time. Brown, official-looking, he and she knew where it had come from - the same place as that first fateful letter. But they'd put off looking at it until the children were at school, and then they had just stared at it, lying still unopened on the kitchen table, for another hour.

Eventually he reached out and put his hand on it, the sudden activity making Carol jump. "Right?" he said, questioning. She nodded.

He tore off the envelope and unfolded the letter, not daring to focus on the words until he held it before his eyes, grim-countenanced.

A remarkable transformation took place the further he read. A smile spread across his face and at the same time tears welled in his eyes.

"What?" said Carol, startled.

Unable to speak, he passed the letter over to her. It had a remarkably similar effect. "Oh, Bryn!" she said, reaching across the table for his hand. "Thank God! Thank God, thank God!"

***

Towards the end of the afternoon of that same day, Bryn was at the side of Brightwell Lake, the water lying placid and flat before him dimpled by fine, soft, warm rain. He wore no hat against the weather, used to being out in all climes, so at times trickles of water ran down his face from his drenched black hair. Warm and safe in his waterproof jacket pocket, his hand was closed round a soft twisted gold wire bracelet, something his grandmother had given to him in his youth (to his great surprise) one day - not a birthday or any other notable occasion. He remembered her words: "Here - keep this. There will come a time when you need it."

"What - to sell it?" he had asked the old woman, widely rumoured to have special powers, but she was shaking her head even as he said it, a smile on her deep-lined brown face.

"No. You will know what to do with it when the time comes. In the meantime keep it very safe."

Today, the day of the letter, which was also the day he was close to the end of the long, long history of Brightwell he was telling to his children, he believed he knew the purpose of the bangle.

***

Everyone said that Bryn had a way with words: the man once swayed a whole community to fight against the development of Brightwell. He was glad he still had these powers when it came to entertaining his children...

"Long, long before the great dinosaurs walked on the earth, and much longer before clever little upright creatures with two legs like you and me appeared, the world was a hot and angry ball of red fire...look!"

"Ohhh!" Elizabeth Thomas gasped. Her father had cupped his hands to hold an imagined miniature of this astronomical wonder in his hands, and then pulled them away abruptly, as if burned by its intense heat, deeply pained, and for a moment Elizabeth, 8, saw that blazing ball left spinning in space just as her father had described it. So did her twin brother David, who was sitting on the foot of her bed to share hearing the bedtime tale of the history of the world.

Wide-eyed, they listened on; the ball cooled, land solidified from molten rock leaving just a few volcanoes spitting out fire while first plants, then sea creatures and finally land animals, including great dinosaurs, inhabited the cooling planet, which was now blessed with wide blue seas and broad running rivers, sweet summer rain but sometimes bitter winter snows.

At this point the children shivered, for it was late January and snow did indeed lie deep and crisp and even outside their cottage on the Brightwell estate. And well might they shiver, for the next part of the story was the coming of the Ice Age, when much of the world froze solid even when it should have been summer ... at which point it was time for sleep, with the story of what happened to this new white world promised for the next night. Time for David to go to his room next door, for their mother to come and say goodnight to them, and for all of them to snuggle deeply into their thick and comfortable duvets with the images of the earth's fiery birth and early years still vivid in their minds.

***

That had been the day of the first letter, which followed up a clinic visit that had meant several tests for little Elizabeth. In regretful tones the letter informed them she had a form of leukaemia and more tests and almost certainly some treatment would follow. Chemotherapy was mentioned, also radiotherapy and, at some point down the line, perhaps a bone-marrow transplant if a suitable donor could be found.

It hit the couple much harder, it seemed, than it hit Elizabeth, who bore the long and trying series of hospital visits more bravely than could possibly be imagined, remaining cheerful throughout.

For Bryn, the storytelling was the highlight of each day. It made him forget for the moment their predicament, Elizabeth's predicament. All the same, when he left the children's bedsides it was always with a heavy heart, deep worries and a yearning hope that everything would be all right eventually.

***

By March, they had merely reached the middle of the Ice Age, for the interim story of the dinosaurs had been requested in full,

159

especially by David, who wanted to know the characteristics and behaviour of every type, from fierce little bird-like running raptor lizards to the armour-headed three-horned Triceratops, the enormous lumbering Brontosaurus, fearsome flesh-ripping Tyrannosaurus, and great flapping Pterodactyls sweeping the skies.

It was now ten years on from the draining of the lake and in that time Bryn had married Carol Cook, whose older son Mike was a journalist in the nearby town where he now lived with his girlfriend, Vicky Price. As a boy Mike had been the finder of Nudd's Hound, the pre-Roman figurine that had proved an especially important talisman for Brightwell Estate and the cottage where the Thomases now lived - the manor house and much of the original surrounds, once under threat from encroaching housing development, had been transformed into an important healing centre, keeping all of its attractive elements intact. Michael Tipton, the Earl who had owned it - a Second World War hero and a good friend of Bryn Thomas - had died four years earlier, but not before giving the newlywed Thomases a special deal on an estate house that had once been two farm workers' dwellings. And Bryn also got a job - estate co-caretaker along with Tipton's widow, Helen. It was not the menial job it might sound, and it left Bryn free to continue exploring the area's past, which had become a passion and the subject of a book he was steadily compiling. It was a big regret of Bryn's that he had not been able to show the earl the finished work before he died. However, they had enjoyed many hours discussing the estate's colourful past.

***

"Now let's see, where was I?"

He always, always started like this, and the children wriggled with excitement.

"After the Ice Age!" They said together in chorus, David adding, "I was getting warmer - remember?"

Their father smiled; once again he had them in the palm of his hand. "Ah, yes. Well, the ice is going. North, north, north it retreats, further and further with every summer, while green starts to creep up the deep valleys the glaciers once scraped in the ground: grasses at first, then flowers arriving with seeds blown by the wind like thistledown or carried in by birds."

"Birds?" queries Elizabeth. "Where did they come from? I thought everything had died of cold."

"No, no no," Bryn corrected her. "You must not think that. Further south in the tropics there were still warm lands like Africa, only I don't think it was Africa then. And birds can go wherever they want, remember?" he flapped his arms and did a little dance. "Free as birds. And up the rivers came fish; the seas were still warm and full of life. And then, after a while, animals too once they realised the land now offered them food and shelter, and the winters were not so harsh."

"And people?" asked David. His father shook his head.

"No. Not for a good while. Although..."

"Although what?" said Elizabeth, sensing mystery behind the word. "There were people then, you think?"

"Not exactly."

"What then? What do you mean, not exactly?"

There was a pause for as moment, than Bryn said: "I think there were guardians too, beings if you like that encouraged and protected all this life spreading northwards, watching, helping."

"Little people, you mean - fairies," suggested Elizabeth, but he again shook his head.

"Things we cannot see or give a proper shape to - life forces if you like, something that's at work in everything, connecting everything to everything else, even in the rocks and stones, even in the ice - yes, even in the retreating ice. And when the first people did come along they realised this and were much closer to it. Spirits are in everything. And they still are, we are all part of the whole of creation and all responsible for its wellbeing as well as for our own wellbeing and the lives of those around us, even if some of us are out of touch."

"Spirits? Here in Brightwell?" said Elizabeth.

Bryn looked at both sets of wide eyes.

"*Especially* here in Brightwell."

2. A Discovery

The crystal liquid trickling down from an icicle hanging below a small waterfall had the fugitive taste and smell of pure water. Panter smiled, caught some in his cupped hand and lapped it to soothe his dry throat. Then he let the rest slip through his fingers into the rime-edged rivulet he was following. Somewhere ahead was the source, which was perhaps where the deer he had wounded was also headed. Stocky and full-bearded, the lone hunter carried on tracking it, picking his way silently through thick hazels on gently rising ground, taking care not to tread in pockets of frozen water that could make a crack louder than any breaking twig.

It was mid-morning, and the early birdsong had ceased. The little summer day-singing birds would not be long coming now that it was getting warmer, but they had not yet arrived. However, as the frost melted off the greening underfoot vegetation he could see that spring was advancing steadily. And here and there, dotted on the frosty leaves, a spot of crimson blood led him on, all his senses alert.

He was annoyed with himself for wounding the young doe when he should have made a clean kill. Something had spooked it at the last minute, while his flint-tipped spear was in flight, and instead of hitting its mark just under the shoulder of the animal where it would find its heart, it instead struck it on the rear flank, penetrated, and then fell away as it sprang for cover. The deer was limping, but how badly wounded it was he could not tell. Having made the strike, it was his duty to find out. The need for food was ever-present but he was also motivated by the thought, a hunter's creed, that you should not leave a wounded animal to fend for itself. If his spear blow had been fatal but likely to induce a long, lingering and painful death, he at least owed his prey a swift and merciful end. And as if this self-censure was not enough, he knew others were watching, gods, spirits, to see he played the game properly, with due respect for his surroundings. He'd picked up the fallen spear and set off in pursuit.

Panter knew he was now far from home and was being led even further in the opposite direction, 'home' being the small group of five families that was steadily making its way further and further north along the east flank of a great river that was sometimes visible in the distance from high ground. Mostly they would stay in a place for two years, maybe longer maybe less, governed by how much game there was to support them - wild birds, fish, small animals all augmented by seeds and berries, roots and leaves gathered by the women and children. With each move they would abandon the dwellings they made of bent saplings, slabs of turf and a thatch of grasses. It was as easy to build these as it was to leave them forever. This area was particularly rich, with enough nearby game and pickings to see them all right for at least another year, perhaps longer. And, mercifully, the last few winters had been mild.

Ahead, the tree stems seemed to be thinning, and he increased his pace, only to stumble suddenly on a rounded stone which violently twisted his ankle. Pain shot up his leg and with a sharp cry he sank to the ground.

The pain made him feel sick. Sitting up and fighting to clear his head, he unstrapped the leather thongs which bound his skin sandal to his ankle and slipped it off his foot. The shin was red, and starting to swell. Broken? Who could tell. Even if it was just a bad sprain, this was definitely a bad place for it to happen. Any help was a long way away. And if he laid inactive here in the wood for any length of time he could die of cold - his body had already cooled rapidly from shock. That, or wild animals would kill him: wolves were ever-present, and boar and bears too. His people back in the settlement would miss him and start trying to track him, of course, but by the time they found him it could be too late. He had to move.

Using his spear as a support he made an effort to haul himself up, trying not to dwell on the fiery pain that the movement sent through his injured limb. Upright on his one good leg, he made an effort to put some weight on the other one, but it was no good and he sat down again, wondered what to do. The best he could come up with was making some kind of support to take the place of his useless limb, the spear shaft being hardly strong enough for the task, and in any case his only weapon - if he had to throw it in defence, he would immediately render himself helpless.

Working quickly with his flint hand-blade he cut himself a passable hazel crutch, a right-angled branch of the straight stake providing support under his armpit. It saved him putting any weight on the bad leg. Although progress would be slow, it was the best he could do under the circumstances and at least he could get moving.

Something - he could not quite put a finger on what it was - urged him to press on upstream, where his aborted quest had been taking him. As it turned out he did not have all that far to go: the slope started to level and ahead, he fancied, the wood was thinning. In a few minutes he emerged in a grassy clearing, perhaps three or four hundred armspans across. He felt warm sun on his face. Ahead, towards the centre of the close cropped grass, there lay a small pool, chalice-shaped and no bigger than a jumpable puddle (had he been fit enough to jump). Towards him from the pool ran a little rivulet of silver water. It was not the main source of the brook that he had been following, the larger water still skirting the clearing at one edge. However the bright trickle from the pool joined it nearby. He approached the spring.

Getting closer, he was suddenly aware that he was not alone. Just to his side of the water was something he at first imagined to be a clump of dried grass, but all at once it stirred: it was the injured deer he had been following. Sensing this was his chance to end the creature's misery he moved more cautiously towards it - he would need to be close to strike effectively and make a clean job of it.

Surprisingly, the animal did not move. Instead it regarded him with large, liquid brown eyes as he raised his spear, then turned its head away to lick its flank. That was the spot where the original shot had found its mark, but now Panter could see it it no longer bled. The spear hovered as the hunter balanced himself on his good leg. Then, quite suddenly, his arm dropped. He could not bring himself to drive the point down.

An overwhelming sense of goodwill swept over him. Why did he need to kill this animal when it was clearly healing? He did not, could not. Dropping the weapon and his crutch he sat himself down gently to puzzle over this while watching the deer laying at ease and still licking its healing wound. Then he let his eyes wander round the clearing. What a spot - a perfect natural bowl with the forest rising gently away on all sides, its grasses nibbled short by deer and hares.

He had just turned his attention to the pool at the middle again when a movement at the edge of the trees beyond its far side caught his eye. A shadow resolved itself: a large old dog wolf stepped into the sunlight. Panter stiffened, reached for his spear, and the animal stood for a moment regarding him and the deer. Then it started to trot towards them. To Panter this unfolding scenario began to have a dream-like quality and he felt more like a spectator than a participant as he tensed for an attack.

Had there been a pack following the animal the risk would have been extreme, but because the wolf appeared to be on its own Panter judged he was just about capable of fending it off, even with a lame leg. Surprisingly however, he need not have worried either for himself or even for the deer, which was clearly easy prey. The wolf made instead straight for the pool where, still holding Panter's eye, it lowered its head and lapped at the water for some minutes. Then, jaw dripping, it raised its shaggy head, gave Panter one last look, turned and trotted back from whence it came. Amazingly, throughout all this the deer did not move a muscle, nor did it even appear afraid. Was there something about the place, Panter wondered - a spell perhaps that protected everything from harm, or watchful spirits?

166

He was stunned by the incident, but a twinge from his leg brought him back to earth. Pulling himself closer to the pool, he lowered the red and swollen shin into the clear water. It was cool, although not so chill as he expected it to be. Fascinated, he watched the water bubbling up through a bed of fine white sand. Near-transparent pinhead stickleback fry darted across its ever-shifting floor, as did myriad little brown shrimps. The pool was about a foot and a half deep, and if he stretched he could push his toes into the dancing grains. He found this had a a soothing effect on his mind as well as on his injury, and after a few moments the pain eased. He pulled out his foot, rolled himself to one side, lay back and closed his eyes. The sun was now stronger and warmer. In just a few moments he fell asleep.

***

Waking, he could see the sun was just about to fall behind the trees in the direction he knew would take him close to familiar territory and home. He would have to hurry to reach security by nightfall, and he sprang to his feet before fully remembering the circumstances that brought him to this spot. He looked down at his injured foot, which was no longer red and swollen, and cautiously shifted his weight onto it. Wonder of wonders, it appeared to be fine apart from a little stiffness in the ankle.

Stooping for a moment to scoop up a drink from the spring, he saw that the deer had disappeared, leaving only a little area of flattened grass.

"Fare well," he spoke to the creature that had departed. He took one more sweeping look around the clearing where all things were at peace with themselves and one another. Then he strapped on his sandal, offered a silent prayer to the spirits of the place, picked up his spear and - just in case - his makeshift crutch, and strode towards the woods and the red of the setting sun.

What a fortunate find, he thought to himself. The others should be told of the spring and its healing spirits, not to mention the peace of

167

the place. If they ever had to move on, it would be good to settle somewhere nearby. With that final idea in his mind he threw the crutch aside and started to thread his way through the trees towards home.

***

A century on, the tarry smell of burning pine logs hung stilly over the poolside settlement as it prepared for another long winter night. The community had grown much bigger during the 80 years after moving to the clearing, which had been widened considerably to accommodate all the buildings at one edge and to make the space for animals. The pool itself had been made much wider.

The larger building at the centre of the hamlet had a dual purpose: it was the village meeting place, where all important community issues were discussed (often noisily) and settled. But the hearth at the centre of the meeting place always had a fire burning on cold days and nights such as the one approaching even if there was nothing to discuss. It had a small ante-room to one side with comfortable bunks where up to six visitors could be put up at any one time. And there was often a steady stream of visitors who wanted to take advantage of the pool's beneficial powers, for its fame had spread far and wide.

Some lame, some blind and led by a helper, some suffering from diseases ranging from mild afflictions to awful ailments like leprosy, some mad in varying degrees and some clearly not far from death, they all passed through, all shapes and sizes, all ages upwards from babes in arms. Before the visitors left the village all had called on the powers of the spring in some way, usually by drinking the water or applying it to wounds, sores and disabilities. In return the community was rewarded for its hospitality, Allstone the shaman shrewdly judging how much anyone could reasonably be expected to pay. He was the one who led the visitors to the water, usually early in the morning when wreaths of mist curled off the pool's surface like writhing life-forms: it was then that the water that never froze looked at its most magical and exceptionally beautiful into the bargain. Then

Allstone would help them with their treatment while incanting a special prayer to the guardian spirits of the place, and when this was finished it was usual for the visitor to cast some offering into the water itself, where it was swallowed up and sank swiftly out of sight into the quivering silver sands of the bed. It was then lost forever.

On this particular evening there had been no visitors so far. The seamless grey sky was promising the first snow of winter and the stillness would bring a deep frost. In such weather it was not unusual for days to pass without the appearance of any outsiders. All the same Allstone made up the fire with some slow-burning logs that would keep it going until morning. He swept up the ash that had strayed onto the surrounding flags and pulled the rush matting aside, out of the reach of sparks, then sat for a moment on the skin-covered bench outside the visitors' room and watched the thin curl of smoke spiralling up to the central roof opening.

A tap at the door, soft and hesitant, drew him out of this reverie. He leaned forward, and was wondering if he had actually heard anything when the knock came again, this time more urgent. He approached the door, opened it just wide enough to look outside without letting in any of the cold.

"Yes?"

The figure outside was a man, tall and well-built. He was cloaked, his head shrouded by a cowl, and because of this and the gloom Allstone could not immediately see his face. Nevertheless he opened the door wider to admit the stranger, whereupon the visitor pushed back his hood to reveal trimmed, curled red hair and a full beard of the same hue. Striking deep blue eyes were set in hollows in the face and with a strong, slightly hooked nose, the overall impression was of a man of high caste, perhaps a chieftain. Yet when he spoke his voice was soft.

"Thank you friend. It's a cold night and getting colder. But I trust I've come to the right place - this is the village of the bright pool, I trust?"

169

Allstone nodded. "It is. Come to the fireside. What brings you, tell me?"

Without answering immediately, the man stood by the fire and stretched out his hands to warm them while Allstone fussed around and pulled up the bench. He brought an iron pot of game and oatmeal gruel and set it in the glowing warm ashes at one edge of the hearth, and while it bubbled he motioned his guest to sit, then sat beside him. He raised his eyebrows and addressed the man again. After his initial smile the visitor now bore a frown.

"Well? You are troubled?"

"I am. But it is not for me that I come. It is for my daughter, a girl of eleven years. She neither eats nor shows any sign of wanting to. Your magical spring is probably our last resort. I fear she will not survive many months more."

"I see. One moment please. You must have something to eat yourself."

Standing again Allstone fetched a wooden bowl, a fired clay flask of mead and two small metal cups from the ante-room, served some soup and poured them both a measure of drink.

"Our finest," he said, sitting again. "The wild bee honey it is made from is plentiful round here, and very good."

Allstone had given himself some time to think while he was busy. He'd met this problem before with young girls. It was some kind of hysteria, he had concluded over the years, but its effects could be devastating. Often the child died after losing weight to a horrifying degree, in spite of them seeing themselves as too fat and heavy. And all the grieving parents could do was watch them waste away. Alas, it was almost impossible to treat the complaint even though he judged some fixation of the mind such as this could be jarred along another track if the right key could be found. Sadly, even the spirits of the pool were nonplussed by such behaviour, although on one or two occasions the victims had found the clearing such a peaceful and

170

relaxing space that their minds were eased and they started on the road to recovery. Of course, if the visitor had not brought his daughter along with him a chance recovery like this would be impossible. His only other successes had been to make the patient experience something to taste or drink which reawakened their appetite. He would have to send the man away with advice like this. But first he had to observe the rules of hospitality and, tomorrow morning, the pool rituals - always with some hope in mind that the spirits would be moved to intervene and restore a family's joy.

The visitor spoke again, looking into the distance.

"She is very beautiful. She has red-gold hair that shines with life," he said, stroking his own red beard. "And eyes like the speedwell flower, or a summer sky. But now, sadly, she hardly weighs more than a wren, and is less lively than a sleeping hedge-urchin. You can see all her bones, every one. I would have brought her for you to see but I do not think she would have survived the journey. It is just too far."

His head sank and he rubbed his moistening eyes with his fingertips. Allstone felt desperately sad for him. He also knew what was coming next - it was the question everyone asked.

"Do you think you ... the pool ... can help?"

Allstone picked up an iron poker and stirred the fire back into life, stared into the glow. It would be easy to say yes, all will be well, and send the man home with a false hope. After all, the chance he would ever see him again was highly unlikely, whatever happened. A lesser man might do so without a twinge of conscience. But Allstone knew honesty was the only currency of true worth.

"I do not know. We can only try. To tell you otherwise would be dishonest. That's for the morning however - now you need rest. We must rise early, and our business will be concluded within a very short time, after which I will give you some things to take with you for your daughter to taste and drink, and you must immediately make all possible haste back to her. Do not waste a minute. Do you understand?"

The man nodded, looking at Allstone keenly.

"And what is her name?" Allstone inquired. "And yours, of course?"

"Anghared," said the visitor. "And I am Neoni, king of the Black Hill peoples. We live to the west of you, far across the broad and shining Hafren you can see from your own ridge. Yet tales of your pool reach far and wide. I...I had to try."

Allstone extended a hand and grasped that of the other man.

"Well met, Neoni," he said. "Now, as our guest, you must rest. I will show you to your bed."

***

Leaving the meeting house a little later, Allstone wondered if the troubled visitor would sleep much. In spite of the man's obvious travel fatigue, he doubted it. An icy little wind had blown up from nowhere and snow was starting to fall as he made his way home.

***

The day dawned bright and crisp with little more than a sprinkling of fresh white under an ice-blue sky - just enough to make the village children gasp with surprise when they saw it for the first time. Earlier, Allstone had brought bread for his guest , finding him already up and about. Now, beside the water, the effect of the spring water's unexpected warmth was doubly magical, with long ribbons of vapour writhing into the air then vanishing. The rising sun was painting them the same colour as the visitor's hair.

The pair sat silently for a while to watch the spectacle. A dozen years ago, the community had enlarged the pool considerably, a move not without controversy. Wouldn't this drive the benign spirits away, some conjectured? Allstone was already the pool's keeper at

172

the time, and deciding the wisest way of dealing with the matter would be to sit on the fence, he left the matter for the village council to wrangle over. The 'fors' won and as a result the water was now about twenty-five armspans wide and maybe twice as long. A decorative edging of large stones had been laid which everyone agreed was a welcome enhancement, and a wooden bench had been made near a gap in the edging where carved stone steps led down into the water. This was for pool rituals, but at times when there were no visitors it was an ideal trysting place for young people. In the intervening years there had been no reason to question the wisdom of the enlargement, and indeed the spring had responded by covering the bed of the additional area of water with the same fine sand that flowed from its origin. Everyone took this as a very positive sign, an affirmation from the spirits.

This morning only a lone robin sang to break the silence. The visitor reached under his cloak and brought out something which he passed to Allstone, his closed fingers for the moment covering what he held.

"I brought this," he said, dropping the item into Allstone's hand.

Allstone all but gasped at the small but surprisingly heavy object: an exquisitely forged and burnished figure of a kneeling girl. But to maintain the dignity of his office required a poker face. Nevertheless he allowed an appreciative comment.

"It's very beautiful. Your daughter, I assume?"

The visitor nodded. "As like as can be made. It is wrought from our native gold. Will it suit our purpose?"

Allstone nodded slowly, passing it back.

"It is ideal. In a moment I will ask you to say your own prayer, aloud or in silence, to the guardians of the spring, and then I shall ask you to cast it out there, to where the surface moves - as near to the centre as you can get it. I too will make an appeal on your daughter's behalf. Then we have done all we can here, but I cannot promise you that our appeal will be answered. And although I should tell you otherwise, you should know that in my experience recovery from the ailment you have described is only likely for half of those afflicted."

The man turned his eyes on Allstone.

"You've come across the condition before?"

"It is not uncommon in the wider world, and neither is it an affliction of our times as some might suppose. Wiser and older men than I have told of similar cases, and have drawn the conclusion, like me, that it is some trick of the mind which has thrown reason out of sorts. It makes young girls - they are mostly girls - see themselves in an unfavourable light and feel that fasting is the only solution. Some of course shake this off of their own accord, and my own inclination is that you try some method to bring her mind back into health, give her something which she believes will help her condition and at the same time awaken her appetite, both for food and for life. Let's make no mistake that while she remains in this condition, her life *is* at stake."

"I have concluded as much." The visitor looked out over the water again, momentarily silent. When he spoke again there was pleading in his voice as well as an air of hopelessness. "I have also tried many physics and spells. Do you offer some?"

"You must take with you some of our honey, which is unique because of the flowers from these parts. Also a methaglyn, made from honey and the heather of the ridge. The honey you will spread on fresh bread for her whenever she asks: taste some of it yourself and judge the craving it brings. The drink you will stir into warm water to be taken before she sleeps - it will assist her rest and bring pleasant dreams. The rest is up to her ... and our spirits here of course."

"Can I have faith in them? The spirits, I mean?"

174

Allstone reached out and gripped the man's shoulder to give him assurance. It was hard to imagine what the stranger was going through.

"This is without doubt a very special place where people have received great benefits. You can perhaps feel its peace now, as you sit here. But all we can do is proceed with hope. Are you ready?"

***

When the visitor left for home later that morning, the community was richer by a beautiful gold bangle which amply recompensed their hospitality.

In time, Allstone forgot the incident. However, the following year, at about the same time that the king's visit had taken place, a messenger arrived with another bangle as handsome as the first one. The only message he bore was "thank you". The next year, and for five more years after that, bangle followed bangle. And with each gift Allstone went to the pool verge and prayed a silent "thanks" of his own to the guardians.

3. The Legacy

Passing millennia were kind to the settlement. By the time it was rumoured the Romans were coming it was a sizeable and prosperous village surrounded by farmland and woods, the wild forest having been pushed back to the foot of the downs in one direction and to the marshier regions of the vale below. The rumours of invasion flew and subsided, rising and falling several times until, finally, the Romans did come, muscling their way across the land despite fierce opposition. Tactical superiority made them virtually unstoppable, occupation was swift and within a century it would have been hard to tell the Romanised population of the village by the bright pool from a community of the same size in Tuscany, so alike were they in dress, behaviour and the need to service the ever-growing tax demands from Rome. Roman laws were harsh but life was far from unpleasant so long as you were prepared to toe the line.

It did not take the invaders long to recognise the special properties of the pool - indeed, a steady stream of native pilgrims and appellants was soon augmented by peoples from all of the conquered lands, especially injured soldiers, as well as ailing Romans themselves. The unseen deities of the pool were given additional Roman names, a small temple was erected at the water's edge and before long an avenue of stalls led down to it. Everything from special lucky charms to souvenirs and snacks could be purchased and the whole village enjoyed growing prosperity from the trading.

It had been difficult in the aggressive Roman takeover for the native inhabitants to maintain local traditions, some of which were treated with inflexible repression by the conquerors - espousing any belief associated with Druids, for example, was punishable by executions of the cruellest kind, including crucifixion. However, a hundred years in, mixed marriages were still sternly forbidden by the native elders. This stricture failed to deter Leila Tomas from falling in love with a handsome young Roman foot-soldier, Marcus Montalbano. It was impossible for her to hide this fact for long from her parents, who were of course set against such a liaison, all the more so because they were not only the leading native family in the community, but they also covertly espoused the Druidic beliefs held before the conquest.

Thus, when the pair decided to elope and start a new life elsewhere, the commander of the local garrison (and many others) concluded Marcus had been bewitched, and withdrew many privileges from the bright pool community while he tried to hunt the couple down. The Tomas family fared particularly badly because the community turned against them. In time they too fled, so that when a chastened Leila and Marcus returned, having decided they were not as suited to one another as they first thought they were, the girl found herself homeless and friendless - and heavily pregnant. After a severe dressing-down Marcus was welcomed back to the garrison, much to his relief because life as a fugitive in Roman Britain had proved to be quite harsh. Bereft, Leila wandered about the pool for several days, begging bits of bread here and there and asking unsuccessfully for news of where her family might now be. Then, on a bright spring morning, a pile of her ragged clothes were found at the water's edge, and wrapped snugly within them was a smiling, beautiful boy child. Leila was never seen again...

Perhaps because of guilt for treating a young mother so unfairly, the whole community supported and nurtured her child and took it in turns to foster him. Not long after his mother's disappearance, when all the soldiers had withdrawn to the garrison to listen to proclamations just in from Rome, a shaman in full robes once again circled the lake, now and again pausing to mutter incantations out across the water while scattering awful-smelling purple powder on the surface: prayers for Leila's spirit. Everyone turned out to watch, and never-empty jugs of mead and methaglyn were passed around until a posted watch shouted a warning that the meeting at the garrison was over and their guardians were coming back.

***

The already-beautiful child Ninian, son of Leila, grew in loveliness and charm, and by the time he reached his teens he was the most popular boy of his generation. By now the local Romans were not so much overlords as part of a loosely-constructed community, albeit some of them lived in a rich strata which owned tied farms and hillside villas. When calls came from Rome for such people to rally to the defence of the empire by going home to fight, loyalty was severely tested. Not everyone wanted to go...

At this time also a new religion, Christianity, had steadily supplanted the many gods of the Romans as well as the British beliefs of olden times. Against this background Ninian became the undisputed leader of the village by the bright pool, and as such he found himself fighting to keep alive the pool's reputation as a special and magical place.

But the relative peace that came with the decline of influence from Rome was short-lived. New invaders started pouring into Britain from the East Coast, and then by sea from other areas - at first a wave of fierce and terrible warriors and later an influx of more peaceful settlers, farmers in the main. They were nevertheless determined to make the land their own. By degrees Ninian and his folk, the Celts, were pushed steadily to the West, and although as a young man he led many efforts to fight off threats to his community, his fate was to die an old man in the inhospitable hills far to the west.

The Anglo-Saxons, the new custodians of the community by the bright lake, maintained and extended the surrounding farmland, and as that community no longer had overlords - and as a consequence, no taxes - everyone became relatively prosperous. Small wonder that the long and peaceful period that followed contained very little of note worth recording - this for many generations - and in time became known as The Dark Ages. It did not last forever, of course, and in time there came a new call to arms with the country again facing the threat of a new conquest, this time from near-neighbours across the channel separating Britain from the great and endless continent to the east, the French - in particular, the Normans.

***

When Marcel de Titon 'won' the Brightwell lands as one of invading King William's trusted barons, he recognised an abandoned Roman villa on the gentle slopes of a quiet little valley as an ideal spot to build his own home; indeed, some of the stones from the ruin were very handy for making a start on the foundations. However Marcel made little use of it in his lifetime, apart from checking now and then how work was progressing, since he had duties of court and, inevitably, wars to attend to. In any case, its completion as a recognisable manor house was not achieved for a hundred years, by which time Marcel's eldest grandson Michael had assumed the lordship. In these more settled times for country-dwellers in this particular part of the country, the extensive farmlands in tithe to the manor not only gave Michael a comfortable living but also paid his much-loathed taxes to king and country.

He was also able to make the occasional small allowance to his younger brother Richard, who one day appeared on his doorstep and asked for financial help - and land - to build a monastery. He was no longer the rough-and-tumble boy that Michael had grown up with: he wore the white robes of a Cistercian monk, and like his fellow monks had espoused hard manual labour as a virtue.

"Come with me down to the valley and I'll show you the spot I have in mind," Richard said. "It's by the pool where we used to catch those little trout by damming the stream - remember?"

While not so keen on forking out more money to help his brother, he saw no reason in grudging him the land he desired - in fact, he had plenty of it, and the pool surroundings were of no particular value since they were largely overgrown with scrub and liable to be so boggy in the winter that they were forever pulling cattle out of the mire.

179

"Ideal for creating some more fish pools - extending the pool that's already there, perhaps?" Richard said enthusiastically. "That will sort out your Friday menus. By the way, what *do* you eat on Fridays?"

"Er..." said Michael, eager to change the subject - boar and sheep meats were his favourites, no matter what day it was. "Perhaps fish pools would be a good idea ... now, exactly where would you put your building? You don't want to slosh around in a wet dormitory all through the winter, do you? Especially with all that kneeling and praying."

His brother rolled his eyes, and momentarily at least Michael saw the Richard of old.

He took the monk down to the bog, whereupon his face lit up with excitement.

"Why, it hasn't changed a bit," he said, looking at the stream wandering between brambles and rushes. "I bet we could put a few rocks and turf in to block the flow and catch a few trout now!"

It was, indeed, largely unchanged from their youth - perhaps a bit more overgrown. But it was clear to see that with a bit of labour a large basin-shaped area could easily be excavated - it was said there had been a pool here in the past, but over time it had filled-in as was often the case with neglected standing water. Richard was beaming.

"Now I know why I was so keen to come back here," Richard said, beaming. "It has a special feeling, don't you think? I know we were both very happy here when we were younger, but it's something more than that - a kind of peace you rarely encounter, almost tangible. You must feel it too. Our monastery must be built here, and we'll open up the fish pool again."

"When do you want to make a start?" said Michael, pleased by his brother's enthusiasm and glad that an otherwise useless piece of ground was going to serve a good purpose. "I can maybe find you a bit of extra labour if you need it, especially when bad weather means my tenants can't work their farms."

He stopped short of offering money.

***

The fish ponds had to wait while the chapel and a linked accommodation block were built on slightly raised ground that bore the signs of earlier habitation. Indeed, some of the locals with especially long memories said there had once been the ruins of a whole village here, while the spot chosen for the monastery had once been graced by a village hall.

Throughout the building work Richard continued to ask his brother for financial help over and above the allowance which Michael kept up, but to no avail. However, his religious order was much more forthcoming, and they also provided an architect and master stonemasons to create a very stylish building, held in awe for miles around. And the community grew, so much so that the provision of productive fish pools became imperative.

Once a series of stream-fed small rectangular pans had been constructed close to the monastery, Richard continued to dig away into the choked-up basin in an effort to find out why more water flowed out of the bog than flowed into it, and in time his workers - fellow monks augmented by locals - revealed a pool of clean spring water bubbling up through the earth. Extending the excavations, he soon created a small lake with the spring near its edge, at which point his brother became very interested in the project and lent him even more workers to carry on digging.

"It looks really grand from the house," Michael said on one inspection trip, nodding back to his home on Spar Hill. "Just the sort of feature a fine estate should have."

So pleased was he with the eventual outcome that he actually gave Richard some money to buy young carp from the continent to stock the pools for Friday meals at the monastery.

***

181

At around this time, there was a puzzling visit from a lame traveller who had knocked at the monastery gate asking for access to the "bright well".

The monk who answered the caller found the request curious enough to take the man to Richard who, anxious to please, asked what lay behind the request and personally guided his visitor to the waterside - slow progress, and Richard wondered what hardships he had to endure through a long journey down from a northern town.

"Why, it's well known for healing, isn't it?"

They stopped beside the spring where, despite the warmth of the late summer day, little wisps of vapour curled into the air above the bubbles, quickly evaporating, vanishing. The man leaned his twisted frame heavily on his crutch, keeping the weight off his withered leg, and looked deeply into the seething water as if he expected some message to come forth.

"Well known? What, already? We have only just uncovered it," said Richard.

Now it was the visitor's turn to look puzzled.

"I has been known for years," he said with a heavy northern accent . "Certainly, my father knew of it, and before him my father's father. For centuries, maybe."

Obviously, some long legend which Richard had never heard of was alive in other memories in the wider world. By contrast, none of the locals had ever hinted the spring, long hidden in a bog, had any special properties.

"How does it help you?" Richard asked. "Do you drink it?"

The man, still filthy from his time on the road and clearly very weary, merely nodded, and seemed to be in some kind of trance.

"Then I shall go and fetch you a cup. Rest here," Richard said.

When he returned to the lakeside the visitor had moved close to the edge, bared both legs and immersed them in the water up to his knees. This had given his tired muscles some relief and he was smiling as he took the cup, dipped it in the water. He drank deeply, one cup then another. Then he rested both arms behind himself on the ground to prop himself up and squinted at the still-standing Richard.

"Thank you. I feel better already."

That was a joke, Richard realised, and laughed. Then, serious, he asked: "How did it happen?"

"I was born with it. Some say it was a curse for the sins of my father, but so far as I know he led a blameless life. Would God treat anybody so? You would know."

Richard shrugged. Daily, it seemed, his religion threw unanswerable questions at him. "He moves in a mysterious way, the scriptures say," he said, "But I'm sure you've heard that before."

"That, and a more than few more choice phrases," said the man, and they both laughed.

"Well, I'll pray for you too," said Richard, "Come, we'll go back to the monastery and you can join our meal - you must be hungry."

He helped the man to his feet, but before leaving the water the visitor took out a leather purse, felt inside it an drew out a coin. "That's to say thanks," he said addressing the water before tossing in the coin. It wafted to the bottom and lay there for a moment, bright, before sinking into the fine sand.

"I have been thinking of a name for our monastery for a few years now," Richard confided with his visitor when they were on their way back. "I think it should be Brightwell."

***

183

When the Black Death struck Britain in the 14th century, and later in the 16th, Brightwell water gained great popularity, many pilgrims coming from far and wide to astonish the monastery brothers and prove its latent reputation. Whatever relief this provided for sufferers is just not known, but it is a remarkable fact that although contact was often close there were no plague deaths in the religious community, or even among other inhabitants of the area.

***

Time passes and fortunes change. In the reign of Henry VIII a row over divorce (banned by the established Catholic church) led to a split with Rome that has lasted to this day. Boundless wrath on the part of the king saw monasteries like the one at Brightwell razed to the ground. Many of the religious people from these establishments had fled ahead of persecution, some to go back to the largely Catholic Continent, others to hide for years in collusion with people who did not share the king's views. The 'priest's hole' in the estate's manor house bears testament to these times, and to the forbidden beliefs of its then occupants.

The heap of stones which was once a fine monastery quickly became a rabbit-infested jungle. Pieces of masonry were pillaged to build extensions to the manor house and not a few village walls and pig-cots. In time it became the bumpy lower corner of a field where farmers were cautious not to plough too deep for fear of blunting their bright shares on something hard. But the glory of the lake that Richard had restored and extended was still there for all to see. And although the spring from which it got its name was now far out towards the middle, it was said that in Richard's later years and for some time after, monks kept a little boat to row pilgrims out to sample its healing powers. And after the Reformation, not everyone forgot about that aspect, either, even if much else had been ruined by a king's whims. Much closer to our times, when another king had to hide up an oak tree for fear of his life, local people swore by dipping a bandage in Brightwell Lake to bind round sprains, rheumatism and all manner of other ills.

***

"How old are the trees?"

The question came from Elizabeth - both the Thomas children were full of questions, always. Bryn was glad that they were as curious about the landscape of their surroundings and the creatures that lived there as they were about its human history, for all these subjects were of course related. He was shaping an answer to his daughter's question when David fired another one at him.

"What is the *oldest* tree?"

"Ah. Well you would think, wouldn't you, that the great oaks, the really wide, hollow ones, would be the oldest of all. They certainly look the part."

"The sort King Charles hid in?" said David, awe in his voice because although he had loved the story of England's civil wars he could hardly believe that all this had happened in his own country - in his own district even. Yet he had evidence of his own to prove it so - a lead musket ball, found in a just-ploughed field.

"Just so," said Bryn. "And many of those oaks could indeed be that old, though they were planted to shade grazing cattle rather than hide kings on the run. That's why many of them are in the middle of big fields, rather than in the hedges or woods. The ash trees are the same, but they don't live quite so long - 200 to 250 years. But if you want *really* old trees you'll have to look at the woods round the back of Brightwell Lake. They are the oldest woods because the ground is too steep to clear and plough. And there are two kinds of trees there that were probably around before the Romans came: the lime and the yew."

"Wow!" exclaimed David. "That's 2,000 years ago. Do you really mean it?"

"I do. But you won't recognise the limes as big old trees. Because their wood was so useful for poles and rafters the were regularly cut down, a ring of new trees springing from the roots at the base of the old one. In time, you get big rings of trees which all look like individuals but are in fact all one self-regenerating plant. But the yews aren't the same as that. They just grow really, really slowly."

"And they made longbows out of yew, didn't they? For the bowmen of England. To fight the Welsh savages."

They all laughed at the joke, which was of course on Bryn and his Welsh ancestry.

"But what about the chestnut tree in the old village?" Elizabeth piped up. "It's huge. It must be really, really old. I wonder who planted that?"

"Oh, a couple of hundred years or so I expect," said Bryn. "There probably weren't any chestnuts in Britain before four hundred years ago anyway. As to how it got there...well, that could be very interesting indeed ..."

The children exchanged glances, sensing a story was coming.

***

Joshua Tipton, a keen world traveller and plant-collector and the great-grandfather of Michael Tipton, Earl of Sparhill, had planted the very first horse chestnut in the county on the slope between the manor and Brightwell Lake. In time it made a fine, spreading tree and Michael Tipton's own grandfather, Sir Roderick ('Roddie' to all in the family) would chuckle every autumn when village boys came to scavenge beneath its branches, taking away hordes of shiny red-brown conkers stuffed in their breeches pockets.

On a late August evening at the end of the 19th century two such lads, Dick Masters, nearly twelve, and Tim Miller, just turned eleven (of local reputation as Miller and Masters, aka The 'Turrible' Two) were laden with conkers and making their way across the village green when they were stopped in their tracks by the sight of a rising harvest moon, ruddy and absolutely enormous, dwarfing the silhouette of the square church tower behind which it had appeared. They watched in silence as it climbed higher and higher. Dick was the first to break silence as the monstrous disc tugged itself away from the horizon.

"Wuh! I never saw such a gurt moon!"

"Is 'um falling down, p'raps?"

There was an edge of worry in his younger companion's voice which Dick (who had seen a similar spectacle before) immediately tried to assuage.

"Nah. Ut'll get smaller when 'um d'get 'igher. You see. But 'um's main close - like we could touch 'um, almost. Look! Look there - a bat!"

An early-out bat did indeed flutter cross the moon's pock-marked face, and their young ears could pick up the sharp 'pik! pik' of its subsonic sonar calls. This, along with the haunting call of a nearby waking owl, caused Tim to shiver anew, for he had heard tales of blind, wild-flying bats getting tangled in the hair of those out walking after dark. This consideration did not appear to worry Dick, and Tim gained comfort from his confidence while the moon climbed surprisingly quickly. As predicted, though still large it had grown gradually smaller, although it still looked sharp-drawn and very, very close.

"Bet I can 'it 'um."

Tim turned to see his companion hurling something skywards and there was the faint whistle of a missile - one of Dick's precious conkers. Strong a thrower as he was, the impossibility of it achieving escape velocity was obviously not a concept that troubled him.

"Yah! Missed!" Tim jeered. "'Ere, let I 'av a go. Bet I can do it."

"How much d'yer bet?"

Tim felt in his pocket for the biggest, roundest conker and weighed it in his hand while he considered the wager.

"All right," he said, drawing back his arm to let fly, "I bet my two biggest conkers - and I gets all yourn if I 'it 'um first. Ready?"

"Uh-huh."

Both looked up at the soaring nut. Tim, as the one who had thrown it, had the better angle for watching it climb to its zenith and hover, almost, on the moon's face before curving back down towards the ground, immediately lost in the darkness. He muttered an oath.

Dick, of course, not to be outdone, had to have another go. And so, in turn, did Tim, while the wagers became wilder and wilder. By the time all the conkers were used up they had lost to each other their treasures, the family pets and chickens and even their houses. Empty-pocketed and laughing like mad things they scampered across the moonlit green to their homes. They were certain to get a telling-off for being late-in for their bread and hot milk supper.

***

Of all the conkers thrown at the moon that night, Tim's first was the luckiest. Some of the others were picked up and pocketed by other children in the next couple of days, while many of those that got as far as the village's one good road were crushed to yellow mush by the hooves of passing horses, and under cart and barrow wheels. Others simply found themselves on stony ground, and by degrees dried out before they had a chance to germinate.

Tim's big, shiny chestnut (after failing to hit the moon) fell in the patch of poch-marked ground in the rough outside the games pitch which was always on the damp side. People avoided it because it grew the fiercest nettles, and cattle were perpetually getting bogged in it when they were turned out to graze after summer's games were over. In late spring the next year, when the hay was taken, it wasn't worth the scyther's effort to go over it. By then roots sprouting from the nut had taken in the damp ground, and a shoot with hand-like leaves pushed tentatively skyward. It slept through the following winter, just another stick among the dried hemlock and teasel stalks, and over the next few years it bothered no-one that it became first a lusty sapling, then a modest tree. Its spreading branches starved the nettles of life-giving light and it dried out the ground enough to enable people to lie under its boughs in the summer sun, and everyone congratulated themselves on being so wise as to have such a useful thing around.

Tim's pal Dick had left the village with his family five years after the conker-throwing incident. The tenant farmer who employed his father had suffered two successive bad harvests and could no longer keep all his labourers. Tim's father was one of the casualties and because agricultural workers lived in tied houses, they were asked to vacate their home at short notice; in the nick of time, by wandering farms far and wide, he found another job, but the family's links with the Brightwell area were broken forever. Although he was also the son of a farm labourer, Tim's family fared better, working for a more prosperous farmer.

In June 1815, he was one of the 50,000 English foot soldiers who helped Wellington win the Battle of Waterloo, returning home from Belgium with no more than a badly gashed leg to Jenny, his wife, and their seven children - three boys, four girls. He'd courted Jenny under the boughs of the rapidly-growing chestnut tree on the village green and they married young. When he returned from the wars somebody had thoughtfully placed a bench in its shade, and he could sit and watch village games from there until he was well enough to join in. A concerned aunt had suggested a poultice of Brightwell Lake water would be beneficial to his poorly leg, and yes, the said, he would try it ... though he never did. In spite of this, however, his return to good health was quick, leaving only a lingering limp. He put his recovery down to being back among family and friends.

By the time Queen Victoria came to the throne in 1837 there were three more children, two girls and another boy, to look after. Against all odds in a world where medicine was still, to say the least,

189

rudimentary, all the children lived to a ripe old age and in turn shared the benefits of the green's splendid shady conker tree. Many of Tim and Jenny's descendants still live in the area today.

***

"Did Queen Victoria really reign for 100 years?" said Elizabeth. Her father shook his head.

"No. I don't know where you got that notion from. But she did live for a hundred years, and she was still queen when she died. My great-grandmother remembered all that."

David said they had been talking about Queen Victoria in class. "At school they said she was still on the throne when she died. Did they really mean that?"

Bryn laughed at the concept. "Mmm, I wonder," he said. "What do you think?"

"It's funny to think about dying, isn't it?" said Elizabeth, suddenly taking the conversation into a sombre area. "Why does everyone die?"

Bryn was surprised how uncomfortable the questions made him feel - not his own inevitable death of course, he realised, for he had come to his own understanding on that matter. The discomfort came from worry about how best to present an answer to the question of one so young. To shadow those lives with thoughts of a hovering Grim Reaper would be cruel - time enough for them to learn that.

"Everyone dies after a long, long time. We grow old and our bodies get tired after many years. We know when it's time to rest. It's not a matter to worry about."

"I'm not worried," said David suddenly. "I'm going to live forever, so there."

Elizabeth smiled at him, then at her father.

"Me too," she said.

Bryn's knife-like pang of anxiety her two words brought passed, and it was time for the children to sleep.

Later that night, however, he found he could not get off to sleep. His narrative of the history of Brightwell had reached a critical period. Entering the twentieth century would bring up desperate wars and awful pictures that were not for young heads to yet contemplate - indeed, he could not himself fully comprehend the horrors of the Somme and what the descendants of Dick Masters and Tim Miller went through after leaving the sheltering arms of the chestnut tree on the village green: young men already tired and laden with 100 pounds of gear ordered to climb out of rat-infested trenches and advance at walking pace, with bayonets fixed, into barbed wire, choking mustard gas and a hail of machine gun fire.

"Did we really lose 600,000 men?"

He echoed the words of the infamous General Haig, and suddenly realised that he was fully awake and had spoken the words out aloud.

Carol stirred, and then her arm snaked round him.

"Of course, dear," she said sleepily. "Now snuggle down and we'll talk about it in the morning."

***

"Now, where was I? Ah, I remember - they were bad wars, and a lot of people died, perhaps unnecessarily."

He'd sketched out the conflicts for them with the emphasis on tales of bravery and courage rather than dwelling on the awful casualty figures, and he was glad that they did not want to linger on the subject other than David volunteering that he'd have been a fighter pilot or perhaps a navy commander, and Elizabeth too professing a preference for active service rather than the nursing and homekeeping roles most women seemed to have to accept - although being a secret agent parachuted into occupied France was an appealing prospect.

191

"And after the end, and the big party that followed, we come to a very interesting period where people I actually know told me what happened to them. And later I came to Brightwell. And here I stayed, as you know."

He did not speak the last few words without asking himself why he had stayed in this particular place. It was something he had tried to convey to Michael Tipton long ago. Now he knew, of course - it was for Elizabeth's sake. Acting on the letter they had received that morning, a letter which told them his beautiful girl was showing the best possible response to her treatment, he had taken himself to the lakeside with his grandmother's curious gold bangle in his pocket, determined to make it a thanksgiving offering to the powers that looked after the lake and the people around it. Yet, in the very act of raising his arm to throw it, while silently thanking the guardians, something stopped him. He could not carry out the action. He suddenly felt he had to keep the bracelet and, in due time, give it to his daughter for her to treasure. Was it message or just a passing notion that had slipped into his head? He looked questioningly out across the darkening water but it gave no answer, just carried on preparing itself for a long night's rest. Never one to question strong feelings that he was doing the right thing, he slipped the charm back into his pocket.

On his way back home Bryn felt drawn to the hall. Entering the bright, clean white foyer and passing displays of lovely flowers, he walked up to a glass display cabinet that held several small historic items that had come from the ground in and around the house, and from the lake. There were exquisitely fashioned stone arrowheads, Roman coins and - in pride of place - the figurines of Nudd's Hound and a kneeling girl. They had all been offered to the county museum, who accepted but wisely decided the rightful 'home' of the objects was Brightwell. With Bryn's help they had created the display and beautifully-scripted explanations of what each object was and what it meant. The additional exhortation to go and visit the museum to see much, much more was suitably discrete.

None of the smartly-dressed staff behind the reception desk questioned what he was doing there - they were used to seeing him in and around the place. It was almost as if he was one of the staff, so they just looked up and smiled then went on with whatever it was they were doing.

After he'd been there a minute or two, he felt an arm being slipped under his.

"Beautiful, aren't they? I often come and look at them myself."

It was Helen Tipton.

"Have you heard anything?" the now elderly but still lively woman continued.

Bryn told her the good news about Elizabeth.

"Oh, Bryn," she said. "I'm so, so happy for you and your family. Michael would be so pleased."

She looked back at the display.

"I'm glad they never left the estate."

"Me too," said Bryn.

***

"Did your great-gran really rake the fire with her hands?"

David's question came out of the blue - it was something Bryn had merely mentioned once or twice as the family sat before an open fire on winter nights. Why he chose this moment of all times to raise the subject Bryn had no idea.

"She did. She was a wise old woman, and she knew more than any of us all put together. She was really special. But I hope you don't try it yourselves because I think we've just run out of sticking plasters."

"But she knew about spirits, that sort of thing you said. And you told us you could feel them around us here too. So perhaps we can as well."

193

"I hope so," said Bryn. "Keep an open mind. Look, our ancestors knew all about such things, and the places they can be found. Think back about the history of Brightwell and all that has happened here - first, the hunters and the spring, then the monastery, and the offerings from the past that were dug up here, and the healing centre we've got today. Don't forget either that the mansion was made into a hospital during the Second World War, helping lots of wounded American soldiers get their lives back. It all links together, doesn't it?"

David nodded and Elizabeth looked thoughtful.

"What became of all the offerings that people put in the spring - there must be hundreds and hundreds of things, money, everything. You've only found a few things."

Not so easy to answer. What came to Bryn's mind was: "Well, what was given to the spirits belongs to them. And I guess what was found was meant to be found, perhaps as a reminder that this is a very special place." Nevertheless, his little daughter was probably right: there was a host of material hidden in the depths, without a doubt - material he felt no urge to disturb now that he had a clear picture of how the past had shaped the present and would continue to shape the future, hopefully for the best so far as his children were concerned. On his computer, this fascinating story was taking shape, the history of Brightwell that he had promised to the late Michael Tipton.

"And are there any bad spirits here too?" Elizabeth said.

Again, he had to think. "No," he said eventually, "I can honestly say I don't think there are. Just good ones ... and they seem to touch everything that has gone on here, make it happen."

"Like my big brother Mike finding Nudd's hound?" said Elizabeth.

Bryn nodded. "And old Tipton surviving the last war and coming back here to save it from being developed and buried in tar and bricks and concrete. And Mike catching a big carp. And the success of the Gobblemouth adventure - have I told you about that?"

194

"Gobblemouth. He was the giant catfish that went to France, wasn't he? And wasn't that where Mike met Vicky?" Elizabeth asked, hoping for another story to spring from this. She wasn't disappointed.

It was indeed where their half-brother Mike had met his future wife Vicky, Bryn told them. The pair had married two years ago and now had a son of their own and another baby on the way. They lived not far away and David and Elizabeth loved them every bit as much as they loved Carol, their own mother, and Bryn, their father. Sometimes all of them met up together for a party, and the special occasions were guaranteed to be fun for all concerned.

"But the fish went further than France," added Bryn, warming up. "Much further, in fact. The scheme was dreamed up by a bunch of crazy old men, but in their own way they felt they were doing the right thing, taking the creature back to his native river. I'll come to the whys and wherefores of the story in a moment, but you know it wasn't an easy ride for the fish or the people who went along. At times things became quite desperate."

"Desperate? How?" David interrupted.

"Well, for example, somewhere right in the middle of France, the tanker in which they carried Gobblemouth and quite a lot of other fish too just vanished - completely! Poof! Gone! Imagine how they felt. And then imagine how much worse they felt when your big brother Mike said: 'I say, can anyone smell frying fish?' "

"Ooohh!" said Elizabeth, imagining. "What happened next?"

THE END

195

Printed in Great Britain
by Amazon

80982583R10112